My inner sanctum

My bedroom was my i   books, my radio—whic   when I was there—and the other symbols of my rebellion: tie-dye t-shirts, Indian headbands and jewelry that made music when I moved; a stick of patchouli incense burning on its wooden stands. My mother decorated the rest of the place in what I referred to as Early Puerto Rican: a religious print in every room.

I had removed my Guardian Angel from my wall, the one depicting a winged creature in flowing robes leading a little girl and boy over the rickety bridge. . . . My mother put the picture up in the hallway, right in front of my bedroom door so that I'd have to see it coming in and out. It came to be a symbol for me of our relationship. . . .

———⊷◈⊶———

"Full of rich descriptions of childhood spent in the barrios of New Jersey, and of a culture foreign to many, but nevertheless fascinating."   —*VOYA*

"A spirited multigenre collection from the viewpoint of young people coming of age in a troubling world. The revolution depicted is part of the human condition, the rough change from child to adult, couched in the bright colors of the barrio."
—Susan Swarthout

OTHER PENGUIN PUTNAM BOOKS YOU MAY ENJOY

The Year of Our Revolution

New and Selected Stories and Poems

Judith Ortiz Cofer

PUFFIN BOOKS

This volume is made possible through grants from the National Endowment for the Arts (a federal agency), Andrew W. Mellon Foundation, and the City of Houston through The Cultural Arts Council of Houston, Harris County.

PUFFIN BOOKS
Published by the Penguin Group
Penguin Putnam Books for Young Readers,
345 Hudson Street, New York, New York 10014, U.S.A.
Penguin Books Ltd, 27 Wrights Lane, London W8 5TZ, England
Penguin Books Australia Ltd, Ringwood, Victoria, Australia
Penguin Books Canada Ltd, 10 Alcorn Avenue, Toronto, Ontario, Canada M4V 3B2
Penguin Books (N.Z.) Ltd, 182-190 Wairau Road, Auckland 10, New Zealand

Penguin Books Ltd, Registered Offices: Harmondsworth, Middlesex, England

First published in the United States of America by Piñata Books,
an imprint of Arte Público Press, 1998
Published by Puffin Books,
a division of Penguin Putnam Books for Young Readers, 2000

1 3 5 7 9 10 8 6 4 2

Copyright © Judith Ortiz Cofer, 1998, 2001
All rights reserved

Puffin Books ISBN 0-14-130974-1

Printed in the United States of America

For my family, here and on the Island

Take me disappearin' through the smoke rings of my mind,
Down the foggy ruins of time . . .
—Bob Dylan, "Mister Tambourine Man"

Contents

María Elena/Mary Ellen

Love and *Vida*

Maria Elena/Mary Ellen

Origen

What we want to know:
In the unimaginable moment
of the union of parental flesh,
was there love, or
are we the heirs of carelessness?
This matters,
That we were wanted; called forth
to fulfill a wish.
That we were meant to be.

$\mathcal{V}$olar

At twelve I was an avid consumer of comic books—*Supergirl* being my favorite. I spent my allowance of a quarter a day on two twelve-cent comic books or a double issue for twenty-five. I had a stack of *Legion of Super Heroes and Supergirl* comic books in my bedroom closet that was as tall as I. I had a recurring dream in those days: that I had long blonde hair and could fly. In my dream I climbed the stairs to the top of our apartment building as myself, but as I went up each flight, changes would be taking place. Step by step I would fill out: my legs would grow long, my arms harden into steel, and my hair would magically go straight and turn a golden color. Of course, I would add the bonus of breasts, but not too large; Supergirl had to be aerodynamic, and sleek and hard as a super-sonic missile. Once on the roof, my parents safely asleep in their beds, I would get on tip-toe, arms out-stretched in the position for flight, and jump out of my fifth-story-high window into the black lake of the sky. From up there, over the rooftops, I could see everything, even beyond the few blocks of our barrio; with my x-ray vision I could look inside the homes of people who interested me.

Once I saw our landlord, whom I knew my parents feared, sitting in a treasure-room dressed in an ermine coat and a large gold crown. He sat on the floor count-ing his dollar bills. I played a trick on him. Going up to his building's chimney, I blew a little puff of my super-breath into his fireplace, scattering his stacks of money so that he had to start counting all over again.

I could more or less program my Supergirl dreams in those days by focusing on the object of my current obsession. This way I saw into the private lives of my neighbors, my teachers, and in the last days of my childish fantasy and the beginning of adolescence, into the secret rooms of the boys I liked. In the mornings I'd wake up in my tiny bedroom with its incongruous—at least in our tiny apartment—white "princess" furniture my mother had chosen for me, and find myself back in my body; my tight curls still clinging to my head, my skinny arms and legs and flat chest unchanged.

In the kitchen my mother and father would be talking softly over a *café con leche*. She would come "wake me" exactly forty-five minutes after they had gotten up. It was their time together at the beginning of each day, and even at an early age I could feel their disappointment if I interrupted them by getting up too early. So I would stay in my bed recalling my dreams of flight, perhaps planning my next flight. In the kitchen they would be discussing events in the barrio. Actually, my father would be carrying that part of the conversation; when it was her turn to speak she would, more often than not, try shifting the topic toward her desire to see her *familia* on the Island: How about a vacation in Puerto Rico together this year, *querido?* We could rent a car, go to the beach. We could . . . And he would answer patiently, gently: *Mi amor,* do you know how much it would cost for all of us to fly there? It is not possible for me to take the time off . . . *Mi vida,* please understand . . . And I knew that soon she would rise from the table. Not abruptly. She would light a cigarette and look out the kitchen window. The view was of a dismal alley that was littered with refuse thrown from windows. The space was too narrow for anyone larger than a skinny child to enter safely, so it was never cleaned. My mother would check the time on the clock over her sink, the one with a prayer for patience and grace written in Spanish. A birthday gift. She would see that it was time to wake me. She'd sigh deeply and say the same thing the view from her kitchen window always inspired her to say: *"Ay, si yo pudiera volar."*

$\mathcal{F}$ulana

She was the woman with no name. The blank filled in
with Fulana in the presence of children.
But we knew her—she was the wild girl
we were not allowed to play with,
who painted her face with her absent mother's make-up,
and who always wanted to be "wife"
when we played house. She was bored
with other games, preferred to turn the radio loud
to songs about women and men
loving and fighting to guitar, maracas, and drums.
She wanted to be a dancer on the stage,
dressed in nothing but yellow feathers.

And she would grow up careless as a bird,
losing contact with her name during the years
when her body was light enough to fly.
But when gravity began to pull her down
to where the land animals chewed the cud
of domestic routine, she was a different
species. She had become Fulana, the creature
bearing the jagged scars of wings on her back,
whose name should not be mentioned
in the presence of impressionable little girls
who might begin to wonder about flight,
how the houses of their earth-bound mothers,
the fields and rivers, and the schools and churches
would look from above.

Kennedy in the Barrio

My sixth-grade class had been assigned to watch the Kennedy inauguration on television, and I did, at the counter of Puerto Habana, the restaurant where my father worked. I heard the Cuban owner Larry Reyes say that an Irish Catholic being elected meant that someday an *hispano* could be president of the United States, too. I saw my father nod in automatic agreement with his boss, but his eyes were not on the grainy screen; he was concerned with the food cooking in the back and with the listless waitress mopping the floor. Larry Reyes turned his attention to me then and raised his cup as if to make a toast: "Here's to a *puertorriqueño* or *puertorriqueña* president of the United States," he laughed, not kindly, I thought. "Right, Elenita?"

I shrugged my shoulders. Later my father would once again reprimand me for not showing Mr. Reyes the proper amount of respect.

Two years and ten months later, I would run to Puerto Habana on a cold Friday afternoon to find a crowd around the television set. Many of them, men and women alike, were sobbing like children. *"Dios mío, Dios mío,"* they kept wailing. A group of huddling women tried to embrace me as I made my way to my parents, who were holding each other tightly, apart from the others. I slipped in between them. I smelled her scent of castile soap, *café con leche* and cinnamon; I inhaled his mixture of sweat and Old Spice cologne—a man-smell that I was afraid to like too much.

That night at Puerto Habana Larry Reyes and my father served free food. Both of them wore black armbands. My mother cooked and I bused tables. An old woman started reciting the rosary aloud, and soon practically everyone was kneeling on that hard linoleum floor, praying and sobbing for our dead president. Exhausted from the outpouring of public grief and exasperated by the displays of uncontrolled emotion I had witnessed that day, the *ay benditos*, the kisses and embraces of strangers I had had to endure, I asked if I could go home early. For the first time, my vigilant mother trusted me to walk alone at night without the usual lecture about the dangers of the streets. The dark, empty silence of our apartment gave me no solace, and in a turmoil of emotions I had never experienced before, I went to sleep the night of the day President Kennedy died. I rose the next day to a world that looked the same.

Lost Relatives

In the great diaspora
of our chromosomes,
we've lost track of one another.
Living our separate lives,
unaware of the alliance of our flesh,
we have at times recognized
our kinship through the printed word:
Classifieds, where we trade our lives
in two-inch columns;
Personals, straining our bloodlines
with our lonely hearts; and
Obituaries, announcing a vacancy
in our family history
through names that call us home
with their familiar syllables.

Gravity

My bedroom was my inner sanctum where I kept my books, my radio—which was always on when I was there—and the other symbols of my rebellion: tie-dye t-shirts, Indian headbands and jewelry that made music when I moved; a stick of patchouli incense burning on its wooden stand. My mother decorated the rest of the place in what I referred to as Early Puerto Rican: a religious print in every room. I had removed my Guardian Angel from my wall, the one depicting a winged creature in flowing robes leading a little girl and boy over the rickety bridge. (The children appeared to be as oblivious to their guardian as to the dark abyss opening up beneath them.) I was taking a stand by refusing to decorate with angels and saints, and by disdaining everything my parents loved. My mother put the picture up in the hallway, right in front of my bedroom door so that I'd have to see it coming in and out. It came to be a symbol for me of our relationship in those days.

Evenings she'd sit in her rocking chair in the living room and listen to record albums she bought on the Island during our yearly visits to her mother's home: Celia Cruz, Felipe Rodríguez, and the big band music of Tito Puente, which she played loud to compete with my Little Richard, the Supremes, Dylan and, later, the Beatles, the Beatles, the Beatles. When my father came home we both turned down the volume. He had to listen to the *vellonera*, a monstrous juke-box going all day long at the restaurant where he worked for the "magnanimous" Mr. Larry Reyes. My mother and father thought everything he did was inspired, including naming the place Puerto Habana to please both his Puerto Rican and Cuban clientele. Papi had to endure listening to the same popular records played over and over by the regulars. When he came home he expected two things: that the music be kept down and that we all sit down to dinner together.

It was my clothes that visibly upset him. He could not keep himself from staring at my waist-long hair worn loose and wild but encircled, for decoration, by a headband embroidered in Navajo designs. I also wore bell-bottom blue jeans torn and faded just right, and the orange sunburst tie-dye t-shirts, once his undershirts, in fact, which I had borrowed from the clothesline to experiment with. This is how I was dressed on New Year's Eve, 1965. In my room, Dylan's "The Times They Are A-Changin'" was playing softly on the radio.

I knew that my rebel disguise worried my parents, but we had an unspoken agreement we all understood would be revoked if they objected too much to my hippie clothes and loud music. By day I looked and acted like a good Catholic girl, wearing my Queen of Heaven High School uniform of gray plaid wool, penny-loafers with socks, hair in a braid, the whole bit. After school I became whoever and whatever I wanted.

I felt that the sacrifice of my ideals for eight hours was worth it to be around Sister Mary Joseph, the counter-culture nun who fed us revolutionary literature and Eastern philosophy under the guise of

teaching English literature. I was getting an e.
education at the Catholic school although I f
more a part of the mostly Irish student body than I
at Public School Number 16 in my barrio, among "m,
own kind." But at Queen of Heaven I was at least free
from barrio pressures, even if never asked to join the
sororities or invited to parties. And even this was
changing as the *Movement* infected the clean-cut
crowds. Sister Mary Joseph had started a café in an
unused basement room where on Fridays, four or five
of us *hairier* students met with her to listen to the exot-
ic records she brought—music to feed our souls:
Gregorian chants, Tibetan drums and bells, poets
reading their doomsday verses in funereal tones to the
rhythms of lyres. We sat in the lotus position and med-
itated or talked excitedly about "the Revolution."

I had fallen for one of the boys, a tall, thin,
black-haired nascent poet named Gerald who wore a
purple beret that matched the dark circles under his
eyes. He looked like my idea of a poet. He would later
become known in our crowd for being the only one
among us to go to Woodstock. The *trip* would cost him:
LSD would leave him so disconnected that he would
have to spend six months in a "home." But the aura of
the "event" he would bring back was perhaps worth the
high price to Gerald—we'd remember him as the only
one among us who witnessed the phenomenon of
Woodstock firsthand. But that was still years away.
When I had my crush on him, Gerald's rebellion was
still in its pupa stage. At school we shared our poems
and fueled each other's intensity.

at first scorned by the other kids. Then,
our little group was self-sufficient, even
asked about what we did in the
and wanted to be taken there. Once we
opened it up to the "others," the club lost some of its
intimacy and mystery, but it widened the circle of my
social life too.

I could never ask any of my friends over to our
apartment. They would have suffered culture shock.
So I divided myself into two people—actually three, if
you counted the after-school hippie version as a separate identity. It was not always easy to shuffle out of my
visionary self and into the binding coat of propriety
the Puerto Rican girl was supposed to wear, although
my parents were more understanding than others in
our barrio.

That New Year's Eve, we were supposed to attend
the annual party at the restaurant, Puerto Habana.
That meant my father would be stuck behind the bar
serving Budweisers and rum-and-cokes all night. My
mother would play hostess for the owner, Mr. Reyes,
who would be busy accepting everyone's gratitude and
good wishes. I knew I was not dressed appropriately for
the occasion, but I was looking to expand my horizons
in the new year with a few new brazen acts of rebellion.

"Elenita," my mother began as she cleared the
table, "did you forget about the fiesta tonight?"

"No, María Elena, I did not forget about the fiesta
tonight." (I had also decided to call my mother by her
first name as an experiment in "evolving" our roles.)

She frowned at me, but said nothing about it. I suspected that she and my father had "strategized" about

how best to handle me. "Just ignore her. It's a stage. It will pass, you'll see," I could just hear them saying to each other.

"Then why are you not dressed?"

"I am dressed, María Elena. I'm not naked, am I?"

"How about that pretty green taffeta dress we bought you for Honors Day?"

That horrible mistake of a dress was in the back of my closet. My mother had insisted we buy it when I had won a certificate for an essay I had written in English class: "Brave New World For Women." Sister Mary Joseph had been one of the judges. My mother had bought me a party dress to wear to school that day. I had worn it into the girls' lavatory, where I had promptly changed to a plain black skirt and white blouse.

"It's too small for me now. Maybe you haven't noticed but I have breasts now."

She dropped a tin pot noisily into the sink and faced me. I had said *breasts* in front of my father. She knew I was deliberately provoking her.

He, in the meantime, had gulped down the last of his coffee and hurriedly kissed her cheek, exiting. "I'll be waiting for you at Puerto, *querida*. I promised *el Señor* Reyes I would open early. Please be careful walking there. The sidewalks are icy," he said, without looking at me. He knew how I felt about his boss, the imperialist Lorenzo, *alias* Larry, Reyes.

For the greater part of my childhood I had practically lived with my parents at Puerto Habana. My father opened and closed the restaurant: twelve-hour days. And my mother was always on stand-by, as cook, waitress, hostess, whatever Reyes needed; and almost every day, she was needed. My father thought of the restaurant as the heart of his barrio life. On the other hand, Mami talked constantly about the family on the Island. It was point-counterpoint every day, not quite an argument, just an ongoing discussion about where "home" was for each of them.

Papi's reasons for not going back to Puerto Rico with us varied from year to year: Not the right time, not enough money, he was needed here by Mr. Reyes. It was only years later that I learned through my mother's stories that Jorge was ashamed of the fact that he could not provide for us the kinds of luxuries my mother had had growing up in a middle-class family in Puerto Rico. He felt rejected by her mother and scorned by his successful brother-in-law. His—our—lower middle-class status, actually more like middle working-class level, did not bother him any other time, however. When he talked about Puerto Habana, his job there which allowed him contact with just about everyone in our barrio, he sounded proud. Every other sentence began with his benefactor's name, Larry Reyes. Larry Reyes plans to open the restaurant after regular hours to serve a special free meal *para los mayores,* for the old people. Larry Reyes is sending baskets to the sick ones who cannot come to Puerto Habana. Every week Larry Reyes had a new scheme which my father committed himself to, heart and soul, and his free time. He would be there to serve the old people after regular hours. And he and Mother would get his old black Buick out of its parking spot in the back of the restaurant and ride to decrepit places all over town delivering sandwiches and hot *asopao*, chicken soup Puerto Rican style, in thermos jugs to everyone on Reyes's list.

Sometimes I would go with them and sit in the cold car rather than go into dark hallways that smelled of urine and other unimaginable human waste and decay. My mother often came out with tears in her eyes. On the way home she would tell us stories of how she and her mother had also delivered food and medicines in Puerto Rico during the war: "But it was never like this, Jorge. The poor on the island did not live in this kind of filth. There was the river to bathe in, if there was no plumbing. There was a garden to grow a few things. They would not starve as long as they had a little plot of earth. Jorge, this is not living!" And she would sob a little. His arm would be around her shoulders. He would kiss her on the forehead and talk about how good it was to be able to help people, even in a small way.

Yeah, right, I'd be thinking, huddled in the back seat, the poor people of her dream island didn't have the swollen bellies of malnutrion I had read about in books, nor did they have to drink the putrid waters of rivers now polluted with human and industrial waste in the famous slums of her island paradise. My irritation at my parents' naiveté grew along with my suspicion of Reyes's acts of charity.

Reyes was an easier target for my self-righteous anger than my parents, whom I saw as victims of his schemes. I believed that he was doing these things for himself: He saw himself as the Don in our barrio, the businessman-philanthropist. Yet he never got his hands dirty dealing with the poor. It was always my mother's heart that broke, and my father's back. And our family time that was usurped. I resolved to get out of this system of haves, have-nots and in-betweens that dominated our lives in the barrio. I learned about the feudal system of king, lords and peasants in my history class, and I thought I saw a clear analogy between the barrio structure and the Middle Ages. I would not be trapped in this web of deceit with the capitalist Reyes as the fat spider in the middle.

Since I didn't even have a driver's license yet, my revolt was at that time limited to small acts of defiance, like the one I had planned to execute that New Year's Eve, to let at least my mother know where I stood.

"Elena. Why are you so fresh? If you are a *señorita* as you are always telling me, why don't you act like one?"

But it was she who was always reminding me to act like a *señorita*, which meant the opposite to her of what *I* thought. I felt I was an adult, or at least on the verge. To her it meant that I was to act more *decente*: Sit right so that your underwear doesn't show under your mini-skirt, do not mention sex or body parts in front of men—not even your own father—don't do this, don't do that. To me being fifteen meant that I should be allowed at least to choose my own clothes, my own friends, and to say whatever I wanted to say when I wanted to say it—free country, right?

"Maybe I won't go to this party." I had no wish to socialize with the barrio's matrons and their over-dressed daughters, nor to dance with older men, including Reyes, whose breath stank of rum and cigarettes and who would be crying like babies at the stroke of midnight, *"¡Ay mi Cuba! ¡Ay mi Borinquén!"* All calling out for their islands, and shedding tears for their old *mamás* who waited in their *casas* for their *hijos* to come home. Actually, though I would never have admitted it then, I loved the dancing and the food, and especially listening to the women tell dirty jokes at their tables while the men played dominoes and got drunk at theirs. But I had taken my battle position.

"Está bien, hija."

She caught me totally by surprise when she said in a sad, resigned voice that I could do as I wished.

"You are old enough to stay here alone. I have to help Jorge." She left me at the kitchen table, defeated by her humble acceptance of my decision when I had hoped for a little fight—one that I could have graciously finally lost—though I was firm on the matter of the puke-green taffeta dress.

Minutes later she emerged from her room looking like a Mexican movie star. She wore a tight-fitting black satin dress with a low neck, showing off her impressive bosom—which made me ashamed to have brought up the subject of my negligible little buds. She had her hair up in a French twist to show off the cameo earrings her Jorge had given her for Christmas. María Elena was still a beautiful woman—though hopelessly behind the times.

"Lock the door behind me, will you, Elenita," she said, her voice soft and sad. I nodded as she walked away without a glance back at me.

An hour or so later I found myself looking through my closet for a reasonable compromise between taffeta and denim.

As always on New Year's Eve, my father asked me to dance the last dance of the year with him, and at midnight he held my mother as she wept in his arms for her *isla* and her *familia* so far away. This time I did not just feel my usual little pang of jealousy for being left out of their perceptions. Seeing the way she held on to him, and how he placed his lips on her tear-streaked face as if to absorb her grief, I felt a need awakening in me, a sort of hunger to connect with someone of my own. One minute into the new year—the beginning of the year of my revolution—and it had nothing to do with the times, but with time's only gift to us: the love that binds us, its gravitational pull.

$\mathcal{M}$aking $\mathcal{L}$ove in Spanish, circa 1969

It was my summer of mourning and tears. And it was my grandmother, Mamá María, who changed the ordinary course of my life. She sent me to return a borrowed serving dish to her neighbor one day during the summer I spent with her in Puerto Rico after the death of Papá José. It was there that I met Pito, the soldier-boy, convalescing at home after having been wounded almost immediately upon arriving in Vietnam. I had heard a woman in the *pueblo* call him "damaged goods." When I came upon him that sweltering June day, he was coiled in his nest of pain and anger on his mother's sofa. He saw me first and lifted his head up on one elbow, narrowing his eyes as if the light I had let in had blinded him.

"Good afternoon, Miss Niña," he said in English. I was startled by the deep voice coming from the shadows in an airless room where all the windows were shut. Mamá María had instructed me not to knock, just go into the house and find the half-deaf Doña Bárbara in her bedroom, where she sewed for hours most days. Caught by surprise, I stood there with a dish in my hands as the thin wiry man in fatigues swung his feet to the floor and sat straight up in one motion. His head was shaved, and his skull was a shade lighter than his face, which gave him a bizarre, divided look. He kept smiling at me, and I noticed how big and white his teeth looked against his deeply tanned face. His huge liquid eyes were his most stunning feature, however.

They seemed unnaturally brilliant and dilated, making me feel frozen to the spot like an animal facing oncoming headlights. Finally I managed a hesitant "hello" and stupidly offered him the dish in my hands.

"*¿Hablas inglés?*" he asked, still grinning, ignoring the dish in my visibly trembling hands. I nodded, looking back at the sliver of light coming through the front door, planning my escape route.

"Then let's talk in English. I have to practice since I am going back to *los Estados Unidos* soon." He winked at me. Then he took the dish, grabbing my hand along with it. He led me to the kitchen, where he stood at the sink and methodically rinsed and dried the dish. Afterwards, he opened one cabinet door after another as if looking for exactly the right spot for it. When every shelf and cupboard had been inspected, he sighed and laid the plate down on the counter.

"It is true, you know, what my sergeant kept saying to me in the Army: Spics just ain't organized; that's why we'll never amount to anything in the world. This island will never be a world power, *niña*, because my mother is totally disorganized. Don't get me wrong, I love my *Mamá*, but she believes the Virgin Mary will help her find something when she needs it. Is your *Mamá* like that? If we have no political future, it's because our mothers do not comprehend the basic concept of organization. Do you agree?"

Stunned by the strange barrage of words, I just nodded. I let him lead me around the dark, empty house, fascinated by his rambling speech and dramatic manner. I had never met anyone like him. It was as if he were performing and I had somehow wandered upon the stage and been incorporated into the act. In a lethargy, caused perhaps by the heat or by the promise of a more interesting day than I had been having at my grandmother's, I played passively along.

As we walked around the old house hand in hand, he talked non-stop in both Spanish and English. His mother's old-fashioned pedal sewing machine had been abandoned for the day, he explained to me, because she had to go to a wake. "She went to watch a dead woman. Why? Where is a woman, who was not allowed out of the house during her lifetime, going to go now that she is dead?"

I was bombarded with, but not given time to answer, many questions that were peculiar but interesting to me since they reflected my own curiosity about the lives of people in a country I had left as a child. He brought us to an abrupt stop at the bathroom door. I must have looked somewhat taken aback, because he smiled and made a military-style about-face before he went in, though he left the door wide open. I just stood there watching him from behind, not knowing what to expect, but fascinated by this boy who couldn't be more than twenty or twenty-one but had already been shot and had maybe even killed people. Through a sweaty t-shirt clinging to his skin, I could tell he had the body of a swimmer, wide shoulders tapering down to a small waist, and his movements were like a syncopated dance, both militarily crisp and graceful. He was still talking as he turned the faucets on full blast.

"They call me Pito here, in that quaint way PRs have of giving you nicknames out of love or spite," he said as he scrubbed his hands under the water, like a surgeon about to operate, soaping all the way to the elbow. After drying his hands and arms with a white towel inscribed with a row of numbers, he again about-faced and saluted me.

"My real name is Angel José Montalvo Matos, your servant." He bowed, reaching for my hands and kissing them. He closed the bathroom door behind him as if suddenly aware of having worried me.

"I had to cleanse myself first, *niña*," he explained in a hurt tone, "before touching you."

I shook my head in disbelief. By then I was beginning to feel a little anxious at his erratic behavior and odd words. But I was also excited by him and curious.

"Tell me, *niña*, are you of legal age to be in a house alone with a war veteran?"

I didn't bother to answer. I knew he wasn't expecting answers from me. Once again he was leading me from room to room, talking non-stop and asking me absurd, unanswerable questions. Finally, we came to what I presumed was his room. The door was closed. Pito put his hands around my waist but kept our bodies firmly apart at arms-length. I could feel a kind of electrical current running down his arms and into his fingers, almost a tremor. He brought his face close to mine without letting our bodies touch. I thought he was going to kiss me. And, suddenly, I wanted him to put his mouth on mine, I needed to feel his electric arms around my body. I closed my eyes, put what I thought was a romantic expression on my face and waited for a movie-style kiss. My first by a man. Nothing happened, although I could feel his warm breath on my cheek. Finally, feeling my face burning in a hot blush of shame, I opened my eyes and met his intense gaze and ironic smile. I tried to get away, embarrassed that he knew I had been expecting to be kissed. I was also a little frightened by the wildness I saw in his eyes, now so close I thought heat was emanating from them. He stared intently at me, as if he were trying to see what I was thinking and feeling. He squeezed my fingers until they hurt and I cried out. I pulled away, now really ready to get away from him. I ran to the front door, where I was momentarily halted by his voice.

"Come back tomorrow when you see me close the windows in the living room. *Mañana, niña,* I will show you things in there."

I knew "there" meant his room, the only space in his house we had not toured. I hurried out into the white heat of the day. I ran all the way to Mamá's porch, where I sat down on the cool tile floor so that he could not see me from his house. *No way,* I told myself, *no way I'll go back there.* The man was obviously crazy.

The way the world has changed for women, Mamá María had said to me after my grandfather's funeral, is that in her mother's time men buried women. Women died in childbirth, or of overwork, or of one of the many diseases that men brought home from their vices and from other women—things that you can get medicine for now. It was not unusual for a man to be widowed two or three times and to father several generations of children. But this had changed. Now women had to learn to live without men, since for the past sixty years men seem to be more determined than ever to kill each other in one war after the next. She herself had lost two brothers in the first world war, a son in the second, and a nephew to Vietnam. I now thought about Doña Bárbara, whose son had come home alive from the war. Did she consider herself one of the lucky ones?

Although I had no intention of seeing the crazy Pito again, the next day I happened to be walking toward the plaza for an ice cream cone when, at the very moment I passed Doña Bárbara's house, the window facing the street was shut hard with a report that echoed like a gunshot at siesta time. What could I have been thinking as my body turned towards the battened-down house, as if I was being compelled by a force greater than my better judgement and free will, hurrying towards what I knew without a doubt was a dangerous situation?

He had seen me coming and had closed all the other windows with the same force, as if providing my feet with a trail of sound to follow. Once inside I saw the beam of yellow light emanating from his room and I traced it there. My heart was pounding so hard that I had trouble breathing. Pito was spread out on his bed like Christ on the cross, the same calmly agonized expression on his face, wearing nothing but a cut-off pair of fatigues. A light-bulb hanging from the ceiling swung like a pendulum over him, and his pupils moved to follow its arc. As I ran my eyes over his half-naked body, I saw that running from his navel down into his pants there was a long scar crookedly dividing the smooth expanse of his torso.

I became aware that he was watching me examining him from the corner of his eyes, but he had not acknowledged my presence. I could have left then, but my feet did not know exactly what my brain wanted them to do, since I felt like heading in two directions simultaneously.

"You may touch it, if you like," he whispered, still staring at the ceiling. Although I was certain that he saw me too, perhaps I had started to move away. Slowly, seductively he traced the scar with his index finger to the point where it met his waist-band while I stood frozen at the threshold to his room.

"I think I'd better go," I finally said, not moving.

That's when Pito swung his legs off the bed and into a standing position in one graceful movement. He was one inch from me before I had taken another breath.

"No, *niña,* you must not be afraid of Pito, or of his ugly wound. It's healed. *Mira.*" He placed my hand on his stomach and moved it over the tough cord-like surface of the scar. I was practically immobile on the outside, but I felt ready to disintegrate or perhaps melt into a puddle right there in front of Pito. I had never before felt the mixture of horror and attraction that he was now inspiring in me. Was this desire? I did not know for certain. After guiding my fingers over the raised scar with his own hand, he placed my open palm over his heart. He kept his eyes locked with mine while releasing my hand from his grip slowly and carefully, as if he did not trust me to keep it there on my own.

After some moments of keeping me in this trance of almost touching, he gently led me by the hand to his bed, where he molded my body to his in a total embrace of heads, arms and legs that seemed as perfect and right as the right key fitting in the right lock. He held me so tightly that I had to push away a little to breathe.

"I will not do anything you do not want me to do, *niña*," he spoke with his mouth close to my ear so that his voice seemed to enter my mind like a message in a dream. I felt his lips moving on my skin, forming the words out of the charged air between us. "You tell me what you want me to do and I will do it."

Then he added in a different tone, slightly mocking, "But you must say it in Spanish. I only make love in Spanish. *¿Comprendes?*"

Not knowing what else to do, I nodded.

"Now repeat after me: Kiss me. *Bésame.*"

"*Bésame,*" I said. And he did. He kissed me in my native language until I forgot all others existed.

It was the summer of mourning and tears. When I came home from Pito's bed that day, I thought I had found and lost love in one afternoon. I felt confused about how I felt, and all I knew was that I was sadder than I had ever been in my life. Pito had kissed me until my mouth hurt. He had touched me where I wanted to be touched and he had waited until I asked him to make love to me. And he had tried. It was then, pressing my face to his chest so that I could not look at him, that he had told me I was the first woman he had tried to make love with since his return from Vietnam. He told me that he had refused to believe the American doctors when they had told him about the muscle and nerve damage the landmine had inflicted. It was the same mine that had killed another man, a buddy who marched in front of him, whose body had partially shielded Pito. Pito spoke in a cool detached voice, as if this was a speech he had long prepared to give. He had come home against the their advice, but was considering moving to New York, where he might or might not go through some kind of operation they had told him about.

After he finished talking he held me in his arms for a long while. I tried to comfort him, saying I understood, but I really didn't know how to understand him. This was my first experience dealing with the unimaginable dual forces of death and sex. I wanted to feel sorry for Pito's terrible loss, but instead I felt cheated of the moment I had dreamed of ever since I had first thought of loving a man. And I felt ashamed of my feelings.

Dressing in the shadows, seeing him stretched out so that his arms and legs took up the room I had recently occupied with him, I felt a deep something for him, something I would call tenderness for lack of a better term to name the emotion in between love and pity. But I also knew that I would not see him again. I was sixteen. I did not yet have the capability to give of myself without wanting back in full measure. I wanted romance without imperfections, passion without scars. Pito had awakened my body to its sexual potential with his hands and his mouth, and with his crazy poetry in two languages: that of war and that of love. He had taught me the geography of pleasure. Because he had given this gift, I had really meant it when I knelt by his bed and kissed him on the mouth in Spanish, in the new way he had taught me. I solemnly promised him, "I will always remember you, Pito."

"Gracias, niña," he had answered in a bitter tone, turning his face toward the wall, crossing his arms over his chest protectively as if I had offered him yet another medal to pin on his wounded flesh.

The Year of Our Revolution

Mary Ellen

When my senior year began, I was immersed in politics, passion, and poetry; the three P's. All of them embodied in my boy-poet, Gerald. Gerald introduced me to protest music and the poems of Allen Ginsberg, which had a heady effect on both of us. Gerald also introduced me to my best friend in those days, his sister Gail, who once took off her clothes during a peace rally and was arrested for indecent exposure. It wasn't so much exhibitionism that prompted her to remove her blouse in front of city hall; it was love of life—an exuberance I envied.

At home and at Larry Reyes's restaurant, where my parents worked, time stood still. The Cubans talked of returning to their island and plotted the overthrow of Fidel Castro. They competed with each other in their stories of lost riches, of glamorous lives lived in tropical splendor before *La Revolución*. All of them had apparently been doctors, lawyers, socialites and descendants of Spanish aristocracy. Now, though, they worked alongside the Puerto Ricans in factories and textile mills doing menial jobs. My father served them their drinks at the bar—usually Puerto Rican rum with coke, a combination called Cuba Libre—and listened patiently to their weepy tales of lost glory. There was little else he could do for his Cuban *compañeros*. For our people, however, he could do more: He could spend his own money on them because they were his Island brothers and sisters. People knew how soft he was, and he became our barrio's father confessor and social worker, with Puerto Habana as his dispensary. My mother did what she could to help him in his mission. We stayed poor while Larry Reyes grew rich.

But my world was larger than the barrio. I kept in touch with *my* revolution through the air waves. I took my tiny transistor radio everywhere with me. The New York City DJ, Murray the K, hissed or shouted in my ear. He introduced me to the music of Aretha Franklin, Grace Slick and the Jefferson Airplane, Bob Dylan, Marvin Gaye, Santana, Joan Baez, Jimi Hendrix—the mixed-bag he called *our* rock and roll in an intimate whisper, making it sound as if he were talking about having sex. I remember I had been in the tub listening to his show when I'd first heard the Beatles' *Sgt. Pepper's Lonely Hearts Club Band.* I'd slipped down into the water, up to my ears in ecstasy, wanting to drown in sound. Joplin's wails of pain and pleasure made my extremities tingle. When I saw her picture, I couldn't believe how plain she was. But later I saw her perform on TV and witnessed the miracle that music effected on her. When she was deep into a song, Janis became beautiful. Her voice, hoarse and choked with pain, went right through my skin, and I began to understand the meaning of soul, *el duende,* in American music.

Gerald introduced me to sensuality rather than to sex. He practiced Yoga, transcendental meditation, and the art of massage. He decided that passivity and self-denial were the keys to Nirvana. His thing was for us to sit facing each other in his darkened room while he recited his poems to me. They were mainly chants of words that made his soul vibrate, he explained to me—like the strings of a celestial harp.

"Let's lap the cosmos," he'd whisper hoarsely, his mouth half an inch from mine as we sat on his imitation Persian rug: Our legs wrapped around each other, our arms intertwined, our torsos not touching. This position generated the necessary tension that inspired Gerald's verse.

"Lick the stars, stoke my fire, cross the universe on a white horse, swim the Ganges with me."

The images were enough for me. I could listen to his strings of beautiful nonsense all night. I knew it was a love poem in secret code. When Gerald ran out of poetry, he would chant to me: "Om Ah Hum," the tip of his tongue tickling my ear. "Om Ah Hum."

Then we'd get the perfumed oil out of his bag. He always had his essential supplies with him; you never knew when someone might need the magic touch. I would take off my poncho, unbutton my blouse, which was usually a diaphanous Indian cotton creation with little mirrors sewn into it and other symbolic decorations I had added. Gerald liked to guess what each patch was, each embroidered clue to my soul, by just feeling it in the dark.

"Here's comes the sun," he would say, tracing the design over my left breast, "and here is a daisy," his fingertips following each petal of the flower. Then he'd move his hand towards my nipple under the material: "And here is Mary Ellen, Mary Ellen, Mary Ellen, daughter of sun and moon, child of heaven." He never saw me undressed, but his fingers knew my body. Gerald's Eastern philosophy and his massages in the dark were the erotic pinnacle for me that year.

There was a darker side to Gerald too, and it finally became clear to me, and to Gail, that he was modeling himself on the self-destructive figures that we injected into our unconscious, taking the words of their songs and the needle-sharp notes of their music directly into our veins. Like Hendrix, like Joplin, like Morrison, Gerald became obsessed with death as the ultimate trip. It frightened me when he first suggested that we try a peyote button. He didn't insist when I refused, but I could tell when he'd been reinforcing his mellow grass highs. No longer gentle in the way he touched me, his nails once cut into my flesh. Another time he almost choked me, his fingers locking around my throat until I pried them loose. Frightened, I left Gerald still sitting in the lotus position, staring straight ahead as if catatonic.

The next day he insisted he did not remember hurting me. I showed him the purple marks on my neck, which I had to carefully conceal at home and at school by wearing a turtleneck sweater. He cried and begged me to forgive him. I saw him a few more times, but he was turning inward for company, turning on more often, dropping out of most of his relationships. Gail and I discussed what was happening to Gerald.

"My brother is *into himself* now," Gail told me in her room, where a life-size poster of Morrison, naked to just below the waist, gazed down at us from the ceiling. She admitted to indulging in "groovy" sexual fantasies involving the sexy lead singer for the Doors; his drug-droopy eyes were a dangerous black pool a girl could drown in, and the inviting parted lips a natural wonder to explore. His tight leather pants did not leave much to the imagination, and that was fine. We both knew what Jim Morrison could offer a girl.

"Touch Me" was playing on Gail's turntable, loudly, for privacy while we talked. Downstairs, her mother was baking an apple-cinnamon pie for Gerald, trying to bring him back from his cosmic travels with the aromas of her kitchen. Gerald's father had scarcely spoken to his son for almost two years, since they had driven together into a gas station and the attendant had innocently called his long-haired, pretty son "Miss." Gerald, Sr. had turned the car around, walked back into the house and announced to his wife that the creature wearing a clown suit and beads was not his son anymore.

There had been scenes, tears and misguided attempts at compromise by the well-meaning mother, all of which were met by her son's passive resistance. Her pleas and threats were sometimes rewarded with a sweet kiss and vacant eyes, a flower from her own garden, or the flashing of a "V" for peace. Gerald's spaciness and her husband's silent hostility had almost defeated her. She had at first turned to Gail for comfort, but instead of her darling little girl, she had found a fledgling women's libber and flower-child. Gail suggested to her mother that she leave her square husband and "turn on to life." According to Gail, her mother had instead joined a Bible study group and a bridge club, where other exiled mothers and wives compared their children's terrorist activities and prayed that this rebellious phase turned national epidemic would pass during their lifetimes.

"What do you mean Gerald's *into himself*," I asked Gail. I was feeling resentful about Gerald's new indifference, which he said was really "peaceful acceptance" on his part. This translated to: If I wanted to see him, fine, I could find him; if I didn't want to see him, fine, he would be doing the same thing anyway: getting stoned, listening to "In-a-Gadda-Da-Vida" with the turntable's arm in the up position so that the record album would play continuously without interruption until Gerald left the room and his patient mother came and turned the thing off. The father had bought earplugs.

"Well, Mary Ellen, what it means to Gerald," Gail said, turning to face me on the narrow single bed where we were both stretched out together, almost falling off the sides, "is that he doesn't care about *this* anymore." Catching me off-guard, she pinched my nipple, giggling uncontrollably while I rubbed it. I fell halfway off the bed still managing to give her the finger in outrage.

"Are you on something, girl?"

"I'm high on life, E-le-ni-ta," she said still laughing, enunciating my Spanish name syllable by syllable.

"I want to know what's up with Gerald. Can you get serious?"

"I can tell you what's *not* up with my brother." She laughed again, pointing to Morrison's crotch above us.

"I'm going," I said, tired of her sexual innuendos.

Gail had joined a women's awareness-raising group her first term at City College, and their "thing" was to treat sex as an open topic, to expand their horizons by trying "everything" sexually, which meant that your friends and neighbors were all fair game as potential partners in your choice of adventures. Until the nipple-tweaking impulse had overtaken Gail, I'd felt that as her brother's girlfriend I had safe passage, or diplomatic sexual immunity, around Gail. Apparently, now that Gerald was "into himself"—no longer interested in exploring the universe in my company—Gail had felt she could cross the line.

"Don't be afraid of me, Mary Ellen," Gail's tone turned serious as she gently placed her hand on my shoulder, pulling me back down next to her on the bed. "At this very moment, maybe because I was thinking of the last time Gerald—you know, gave you a massage, I did feel turned on. But I can be cool about it. We can talk."

"How do you know . . . I mean . . . did Gerald tell you . . ." I was shocked that Gail knew about my sessions with Gerald. I had always told her about the poetry and the massages, but, not the other stuff. In spite of my outward bravura and my rebelliousness against my parents' uptight moral values, I felt a little ashamed of letting Gerald touch me the way he did. Because we did it in total darkness in his room, I stupidly believed that no one else suspected what went on.

"I was there," Gail said in a whisper.

My impulse was to jump off the bed and run home. How could Gerald betray me this way? How could Gail call herself my friend when she was a voyeur, a pervert, spying on her best friend's and her brother's most intimate moments together? I surprised myself by just lying stock-still on the bed next to Gail. *And did you touch me too?* I did not ask aloud.

Next to me, her mouth close to my ear, Gail hummed a song we both knew, but did not move either.

Gerald emerged from his dark cocoon enough times to finish high school, although he tested and stretched the limits of Queen of Heaven High's faculty and administration. He might never have grad- uated if it had not been for our hippie-nun Sister Mary Joseph's intercession—and the fact that he was brilliant. He read and understood philosophy. High-school subjects were child's play to him, for Gerald could interpret the words of Shakespeare, Milton and Blake as well as those and John, Paul, George and Ringo. He couldn't have cared less about the diploma, but somehow, even in the recesses of his chemically saturated brain, he must have known that it would undo the last connection he had to his family and to the world if he did not finish his senior year. Also, he saw life as a series of events that you either allowed to happen to you or you passively resisted. He allowed his high-school graduation to hap- pen to him, then he celebrated his freedom by blowing his mind with acid at a rock festival. The unforeseen consequence of his orgy was half a year in the nut- house, paid for by his father's insurance company, followed by the realization that the breakdown had been a gift from the karmic forces of rock-and-roll: He would not be drafted.

Gerald's dropping-out had been gradual, though, and my memories of our senior year are like black and white photographs with a shadowy figure at the edge that no one can quite identify. That was Gerald. Gerald in his ankle-length black trench coat, John Lennon-style eyeglasses and hair down to his shoulders, standing just behind me at the café where we listened to the other young men and women in black recite their angry verses and sing their protest songs. More and more I began to lose interest in the mediocre poetry and the mindless repetition of slogans. My own pupa-stage poems were seeking out the concrete image that would years later give shape, form and meaning to my fragmented world.

My mother never met Gerald or Gail, or many of my friends outside the barrio. But she watched me from her window, and she waited and she knew, maybe through her dreams which she believed in, or by my smell, my music, by my wild look. Or maybe by spying on my sidewalk passions with Gerald. She knew that I was staring down the abyss with my boy-poet. So she gave me a choice one night: free love or her love.

María Elena

My hair started turning gray that year, seeing the turmoil on the streets of America and waiting for my daughter to come home from her rallies, demonstrations and sit-ins. Late into the night, I sat in my rocker by the window, waiting to see the pretty girl with the wild black mane of hair hiding herself inside a huge poncho. I watched her coming down the block, clutching her books and papers, head bowed as if she were burdened with the worries of the whole world. Such a serious child. So intent on righting wrongs that she missed all of the good things that I thought a young girl would want: pretty clothes, fiestas, fun with other teen-agers. I knew that she liked boys, although those years I had to look very closely to tell the difference between the sexes. Both wore the ragged blue jeans, painted t-shirts and ridiculous jewelry. They let their hair grow and wore it wild and tangled as moss on a tree. From my window I could not always tell if her occasional companions were girlfriends or *novios*.

There was no doubt, however, the night I saw the obscene kiss in front of our building. By the light of the street lamp, I could clearly see the entire spectacle. Although I did not want her to know that I watched her in such a clandestine manner, I was alarmed one night to see the groping and abandoned caresses. It was *el poeta*, Gerald, she wrapped herself around one night. The boy looked like he needed a good night's sleep, a hot meal and a hair-brush. I did not understand what she saw in him. Perhaps her enchantment with words and poetry was embodied in the unkempt boy. I knew I had to say something to her about the display on the street. She walked in preceded by the wave of that patchouli oil that permeated her person and everything she touched in those days. It was a pagan smell, calling up for me images of naked people dancing around a fire. I was sitting in the dark living room, so I startled her when I spoke her name.

"Elenita. Please come here for a minute, *niña*," I said, trying to calm myself before speaking.

"What are you doing up so late, Mother? Hey, have you been spying on me?"

"*I* will ask the questions, Elenita." I reached over and turned on the light. Her hands shot up to cover her face as if she had something to hide. But she regained her rebel pose quickly.

"Have you thought about what people in this barrio will say if they see you being intimate with a man right on the sidewalk?"

"You *were* spying on me!"

She was furious, as I knew she would be, but I was determined to speak my thoughts.

"You are forgetting something, *hija*," I spoke calmly so that she would know that I did not intend to be intimidated by her anger. "You live in my house. And as long as you as you call this home, you will answer to me and your father for your moral behavior."

"Then maybe it's time that I leave your *home*," she answered sharply. And the way she said *su casa* hurt me. "Perhaps you haven't noticed, stuck as you are behind these four walls, that there's been a sexual revolution going on out in the real world." She continued speaking in the same sarcastic tone. "People don't have to ask their parents or anyone for permission before they make love. It's a personal matter, Mother!"

"I call what you are suggesting immoral behavior, *hija*. If you are saying that for girls to pass their bodies around to many men is not a sin, then you are wrong. The body is a temple—"

"My body is *my* temple, and I will conduct services any way I want!"

I saw that I could never hope to win a battle of words with my daughter: They were her domain. Even then she could use language to her advantage like no one else I knew. So I brought out my most dangerous and final weapon. Trembling in fear, I said, "I cannot *live* with you if you have given yourself over to a life of sin. I do not want you to go, but you have become a stranger to me."

She looked at me in horror. I knew I had shocked her because she thought that my devotion to her was greater than my objections to anything she could do. And it was. I was playing this game of chance, risking my whole life and my soul—for I could no more give up my child than I could stop breathing—hoping she would understand the gravity of our moral dilemma.

"You're throwing me out?"

She had sunk to the floor in front of my rocker. Her heap of bright rags spread around her, she seemed to shrink into a little girl again. I held back my need to comfort my child, keeping my hands locked together so as not to reach out to her.

"No, Elenita," I spoke firmly although my throat felt constricted by fear. "I am telling you that if the morals we taught you mean nothing, then we are no longer a family. You must make a choice. If you want to live without rules, then you must make a life away from us. On your own."

She sank back on her knees staring at me in disbelief, as if I had suddenly turned into a monster right there in front of her. She had never known that I too could rebel against injustice.

"You don't understand, Mother. Things have changed in the world. A modern woman makes her own choices . . . She has the freedom to choose."

Now she was going to give me a lecture on free love, but I interrupted her.

"Nothing of value to your life is free, Elenita. *Nada. ¿Entiendes?* Not even love. Especially not love. Look around you. Women have always paid a high price for love. The highest price. I am telling you that if you want to be an adult, you have to learn the first lesson: Love will cost you. It is not free."

She sat there taking in my pronouncements. Not in the usual way that people process things. Not *my* Elenita. She was translating and transforming what I had said inside that unknowable mind of hers. And when I would hear my own words again, coming out of her mouth, they would sound foreign to me.

My plan was to walk out on *her* for once, leaving her there to think about the choices I had given her. But I could not help myself. As I walked past my *niña* sitting stiffly in her pagan costume, I stroked her hair. She lay her wild head inside the circle of my arms for one brief moment, then rushed to her room to drown out the world with her long-playing albums. I will remember that night as the beginning of the end of the worst year in the history of parents and children: 1968, the year of our revolution.

El Olvido

It is a dangerous thing
to forget the climate of
your birthplace; to choke out
the voices of the dead relatives when
in dreams they call you by
your secret name; dangerous
to spurn the clothes you were
born to wear for the sake of fashion;
to use weapons and sharp instruments you
are not familiar with; dangerous
to disdain the plaster saints before
which your mother kneels praying for you with
embarrassing fervor that you survive in
the place you have chosen to live; a costly,
bare and elegant room with no pictures
on the walls: a forgetting place where
she fears you might die of exposure.
Jesús, María, y José.
El olvido is a dangerous thing.

The One Peso Prediction

My father died of an unexpected heart attack during my first year at City College. At his funeral, I did not allow myself to be weak like the others. A Puerto Rican funeral is not something I had experienced before, so I had prepared myself. I needed to be in control of myself in order to take care of my mother, whom I had expected to be in a state of hysteria or collapse. But once again, she had surprised me. Though she looked pale and shaky, she had stood up through the whole thing with dignity. That was not so for other mourners.

I was ready for almost anything, but the sight of grown men crying like children as they looked upon my father's face shook me up. They sobbed without restraint and were comforted by the women, whose own tears flowed freely. My mother dabbed at her eyes constantly, but did not break down.

The mass for the dead was said in Spanish by Father Jones, the pastor of St. Mary's where I had received my First Communion, and where we had attended Sunday mass since my parents came to the U.S., one year before I was born. He was an old man now, retirement age, at least, but since few young men were taking the vows these days, the Catholic church was discouraging priests from retiring. Father Jones's skeletal body underneath the somber vestments made me sad. His lifelong devotion to the Puerto Rican community in the city had been, still was, all he had. Once I asked him if he had ever regretted becoming a priest. He had said, "I had as much of a choice in becoming a priest as you had in becoming a pretty young woman, *hija*."

I felt a little dizzy during the mass, and my mother sensing something was wrong took my hand in hers. The nave seemed to be in motion with the soft mourning sounds of stifled sobs and an occasional "Ay, ay." In order to stay focused I began to count the people now framed in a black canvas, to place them in context from other occasions in my life when I had been a part of their world: there was Doña Rosalia who had a beauty shop where women could still get beehive hairdos since her specialty was to re-create the past for her aging customers. I remembered my mother taking me there for my pageboy haircuts as a little girl, and I remembered rebelling against getting my hair done by Doña Rosalia for my first dance. She wanted the daughters to look like the mothers.

Sitting behind her was a whole row of Rodriguezes. I had gone to grammar school with several of them. They were a family of eight children. The Rodriguez elders were fervent Catholics who took the Pope's ban of birth control seriously, or so I had heard my mother say, "As if the Papa in Rome knew what it's like to have a child." The Rodriguez family were, therefore, a neighborhood project, with everybody pitching in when a new baby came or there was illness (epidemic in scope since the Rodriguez family lived in a small apartment and when one got sick so did the others).

The Cordero family was represented by my father's only surviving sister, who had flown in from California where she had spent her adult life fighting for the rights of migrant workers, teaching them English in her own home, which she shared with her Chicano lawyer husband. They had no children, although they often joked about the Chicano-Riqueño baby they had always wanted. They joked to hide their pain, I had always thought, and they worked harder than anyone else. Tía Rita and her husband, Julian, were my two favorite relatives, although I got to see them only when the family got together at Christmas before my father died.

No one in my mother's side of the family on the Island had been able to come to the funeral, so the church was filled with the people not related by blood, but by the loyalty that my father had surrounded himself with during his life. He never had any extra money, but there was always something to give a *compañero* in need. I used to hear my parents going over their usual complaints late at night. My mother wanted to save money and buy a house in Puerto Rico when I finished high school. She had extracted an offer from her brother for a job for Father in the family's furniture store. My father promised her the house, but would not discuss the job working for her brother. Although it had never been fully explained to me, my father had not been the family's favorite choice for a husband for my mother. The fact that they had married right out of high school and come to live in the States had become a source of anger and even alienation from the family.

This had all happened in my prehistory. All I know is that at some point in my early childhood I had started traveling down to my grandmother's house on the Island with my mother. My father never accompanied us except once to my grandfather's funeral.

To distract myself I recalled that trip. My parents dressed in their mourning clothes, and I arrived on the Island to bury Don José, my grandfather. In those days, shuttle service by air had not been perfected and we hired a *carro publicos* to drive us the four hours through and over the mountains to our *pueblo*—the superhighway now known as the *autopista* was still under construction then, the American engineers directing the blasting through solid rock and leading a legion of sweating men down a straighter path across the Island.

My father spoke almost not at all during that trip, but steadfastly held my constantly weeping mother's hand. I, in my rebel clothes, ignored the pointed stares of people, particularly the women who did not lower their voices when they made comments about my patched jeans and black and orange African dashiki. I read Kerouac, my latest "find," and pretended I too was on the road. I had not really gotten close to Papa José since he was almost never at home when Mother and I visited Mamá María. I had heard that he maintained another *casa* and family in the *pueblo*. Of course I felt sad about his passing, he had always been sweet to me in a formal way, often giving me little gifts such as carved boxes his craftsmen custom-made for him, and jewelry that was a little too fine for my tastes back then. But it was Mamá María that I felt closer to, instinctively recognizing in her a streak of rebellion and pride I identified with and which I did not see in my mother.

After the draining ride—no air-conditioning in the car—and two more passengers squeezed in, one of them carrying a cage with doves in it, we arrived at Mamá María's house, drenched in sweat and exhausted. We found her in a frenzy of activity. I watched my mother detach herself from us to become Mamá María's shadow. After offering his condolences and shaking his brother-in-law's hand, my father shrank into the background; at times during the three days he was there even disappearing altogether. Only I knew where he went because I asked him: he went on long walks to the places where he had grown up, where he had met my mother, and to his parents' graves. His parents had died within months of each other during an influenza epidemic a few years after he had left the Island. He had not allowed us to accompany him to the funeral, fearing for our health. Apparently his parents had been much older when they had him—they were in their sixties when they were overcome by the Asian flu. I had never met them.

I slipped out of the crowded house on the second day of our arrival and caught him as he was going out the door. He motioned me to a cement bench in Mamá María's lush garden. It was in a little grove where there grew a tamarind tree with hanging plants in baskets—huge tropical orchids—and rhododendron trailing their leafy vines down and around the bench concealed us like a green curtain. I loved hiding there to read. My father had apparently discovered the oasis, too. There we couldn't be seen from the house, but we had a perfect view of the people coming in and out of the front door.

"This is where your mother and I talked the few times I was allowed to visit her," my father whispered. I knew why he spoke so softly. This place demanded silence and respect like a church. I smiled at him, imagining their romantic meetings.

"Only one thing was different then," he smiled back at me and winked. "Doña María kept her jungle pruned. This was not here." He ran his fingers down the thick vines. "She was not about to let her daughter out of her sight."

"You asked me where I was going, Elenita. For a walk. To see if the past is still there. Don't raise that eyebrow at me, *niña*. When you get older you'll find yourself doing the same thing. The past will matter more and more. You will want to remember your dreams and to know what happened to them."

For once, I did not interrupt. I was used to hearing gentle lectures from my father. But his sad voice and the dreamy things he was saying were more usual in my mother. It was almost like he was saying good-bye to this place, and admitting that his dreams had not come true. He spoke of his parents a little. How they thought they'd live to see Puerto Rico become a state. He added with irony, "And then we would all be rich Americans." He spoke of seeing his María Elena for the first time and knowing without a doubt that they would marry. "It was not easy to convince that stubborn old woman in there to let her daughter marry an *Estadista*. We were imperialist devils to her—the old revolutionary." But there was more humor than anger in his voice as he said this. I knew then that he had grown to like Mamá María a little; or if not to like the woman, at least to admire her strong character.

"Like Romeo and Juliet," I said.

He laughed a little, "Yes, *hija*. If Romeo and Juliet had lived on this island their parents would have belonged to opposing political parties. Fortunately, we did not have to end up like them." He patted my knee, right where I had sewn a peace-symbol patch on my blue jeans. He shook his head and smiled sadly at me.

"Take care of your mother." He got up. His eyes were already on the road. People had overflowed my grandmother's house onto the porch. Doña María was moving among them—easy to spot in her black dress and mantilla. My mother, also in black, followed her.

I watched my father disappear down the street, wishing I could go on his search with him. But I saw my mother looking around. I knew I would soon hear my name called out. My place was with her and Mamá María learning to play hostess to death.

At that time it interested me only a little to hear the women in the kitchen whispering about how Mamá María had insisted on riding in the ambulance that picked up my grandfather's body at his mistress's house, and how the two women had bathed and clothed him together. There was outrage in the tone of one of the younger women when she referred to that "other woman." Then an older woman, about Mamá María's age, had said, "They both loved the man."

The wake and funeral were like a movie in slow motion to me, the outsider, the observer. Soon after, my father told me that he was going home and that my mother and I would be staying at Mamá María's the rest of the month. One month is an eternity when you are sixteen. I protested, but not too loudly, since the house was observing *luto*, deep mourning. Even I knew better than to violate the time of respect due the recently dead.

It was years later that I learned through my mother's stories that Jorge was ashamed of the fact that he could not provide for us the kinds of luxuries my mother had had growing up. He felt rejected by Doña María and scorned by his successful brother-in-law. His, our, lower-middle-class lifestyle did not bother him any other time, however. When he talked about his job in a barrio restaurant and tavern, which allowed him contact with just about everyone in our barrio, he sounded proud. He was proud of the fact that he had talked the owners into opening the restaurant after regular hours to serve a special free meal *para los mayores*, for the old people, several times each month, and to prepare baskets for the sick ones who could not get around any longer. Every week he had a new charitable scheme to which he committed himself heart and soul. And he gave them all his unpaid time. He would be there to serve the old people after regular hours. Some weekends he insisted that I accompany them in his old black Buick, which spent most of its time parked in the back of the restaurant, and ride to decrepit apartment buildings all over town delivering sandwiches and hot *asopao*, chicken soup Puerto Rican style, in plastic containers to everyone on his long list.

I resented his charity work. It took him away from our home. It was my mother's heart that broke, our family time that was usurped. I resolved to get out of that system of haves, have-nots, and in-betweens that dominated our lives. My father was the middleman and we were stuck in the economic and social limbo. When I read about the feudal system of king, lords, and peasants, I saw a clear analogy to the barrio structure.

The noise level in the church intensified as the mass came to an end and the coffin's lid was lowered. I took my mother's arm and led her into the rented limousine. The wind whipped up as we stood around that rectangular hole in the ground, and I felt the hot trails of tears on my frozen cheeks.

After the funeral we went back to our apartment to eat leftovers of the food the women had brought: the rice and beans, and the spicy fried chicken, and plates stacked with *tostones*, plantain slices made into a sort of thick chip. We ignored the festive-looking food and separated. I went into the living room and sat on Papa José's old chair; mother made us some *cafe con leche* in the kitchen, then called me in. I watched her closely for signs that she was breaking down. She spilled a little coffee on the table as she poured me a cup. Her new paleness, accentuated by her heavy black dress, worried me. She was still beautiful, although the lines framing her mouth were deepening. I wondered if I would have the same lines on my face as I got older. Our hands, with the bony fingers and traceable veins, were nearly identical. Despite our physical similarities, our views on almost everything had become so different that I did not know how to begin to comfort her.

"*Hija*, I still cannot believe it." She spoke in Spanish, and I mentally switched over to that language. I had fallen out of the habit of speaking in Spanish automatically. My mother understood English but spoke it only when absolutely necessary; but she used only Spanish with the family. I understood that she was ready to talk about my father, and the best thing I could do for her was to listen. I felt my own grief over my father fluttering in my chest waiting for me to release it. I told it to wait. I could always make my heart take orders from my brain in times of emergency. It was a skill that I had mastered as a survivor in the tough city.

The story of how my father came into her life is one I had heard in installments over the years. The details changed ever so subtly with each telling, so that she who initially played the role of a Latina Juliet ready to die defending her love for the rejected suitor changed into a different heroine according to how she saw me at the time of the telling. I understood the motives for the revisions: as I got older and the danger of *my* being swept away by love became a possibility, the story had to shift its focus to the parents' side of the argument. I had always preferred the original version, the one in which my mother plays the beautiful young maiden held in captivity by her overprotective parents. She is rescued by the love of a handsome young man who will not take no for an answer. They try to elope, but are found out. After much argument and many bitter tears, the mother relents and they have a small but elegant church wedding. The end. The end of their island life and carefree youth, that is. A year later the young couple are living in a cold American city and expecting their first child: me. I know what happens after that: a life of making ends meet and making do with a little help from our friends.

I couldn't help but wonder how the story of my parents' romance would be different now that the young man who would not take no for an answer, was dead. The man I knew had learned to take no as an answer on a regular basis. My love for my father had been for many years in conflict with my anger at his acceptance of the daily humiliations of his low-paying job, at his unwillingness to demand more for himself and for us. I had always made my resentments obvious at home, much to my mother's distress. Loyalty, humility, poverty. The motto on my father's banner. Even after his death I felt like screaming at his empty chair in the kitchen, where he had sat to teach me how to play dominoes, do my math, learn my lessons: "Papi, stand up for your rights. Be a free man!"

"Your father was the only man for me," my mother began, slowing down her Spanish as she did when telling something that she wanted me to understand fully. "Three times he had been predicted by the *madama* I consulted about my future. That woman lived to be over one hundred years old and had divined every marriage, birth, and death in town for several generations. Practically every one. Every year since I was thirteen, I would go to see her on my birth-day. If you didn't have the peso she charged, you could take her something else she could use, like a few yards of cotton cloth or vegetables from your garden. Once I took her a handkerchief I had embroidered myself. She liked it so much that she put it in her pocket immediately. She lived in the country, and it took about one hour to get there on foot. Mamá María did not want me to go there because she believed the *madama* was a fake. I had gotten permission to visit a friend and go to a movie that day. My friend and I went to have our palms read instead. I have never felt bad about lying to my mother about my visits to the *madama* because that is how I knew your father was coming to me.

"But I'll start at the beginning. *Pues, hija,* when I was growing up in their house on the Island, my mother and father were heavily involved in politics. I think one of the first big words I learned to say was *Nacionalista,* and to my brother and me it meant a bunch of loud people in someone's living room, often our own, talking about boring matters. There were names said with reverence, the names of patriots who had had to go into political exile or to prison because they wanted independence for the Island. There was talk of revolutions, of the Cuban struggles. We would stay awake long enough to eat the coconut candy and drink the sweet sugar cane cider. Then the children would curl up in beds or climb into hammocks or parents' laps.

"One day a neighbor woman came to get us at school. She took us to her house and told us that Mamá María and Papá José were at an important meeting in the city of Ponce. They would be home late. But they did not come home for three days. I cried myself to sleep every night thinking that they were dead and this woman was not telling us. When Mamá finally came for us she looked sick. She had a bandage on the side of her face. Crying hysterically, I clung to her. She held us both in her arms, and I could hear her heart beating very fast. When we were home and she had changed her dirty clothes and her bloody bandage, she explained that there had been a little problem at the meeting in Ponce. She had fallen and hurt herself. Papá too was hurt, but not badly. It would just be a few days before he came home.

"It was a long time before I found out about the riot Mamá María had helped to incite with a speech she gave in the town's plaza. There had been bottles and rocks thrown at her and Papá José. They had been taken to jail where she had refused to eat for the three days they had held her.

"Frustrated by the stubborn woman's hunger fast and pressured to release the mother of two young children, the police had sent her home but kept her husband a few more days as an example of what would happen to political agitators in their *pueblo*.

"After that we were treated like heroes by some people and cursed as troublemakers by others. School was hell for a while since it was run by an American superintendent who thought of my mother as a hypocrite for calling herself pro-independence while sending her children to a school supported by U.S dollars. But what else could she do? All the public schools were administered by people sent directly from the mainland. She did not want to send us to the Catholic school run by American nuns. She had no choice about our education. But all *I* wanted was to be an ordinary girl. To have friends at school that I chose, not only the daughters of other *Nacionalistas*. I wanted to get invited to parties without somebody mentioning my parents' politics.

"It was not so much Papá José who caused all the gossip in our *pueblo*. He was an activist too; but as a quiet man, he wanted to change things slowly. I remember him dressed in his election-day white linen suit with a Puerto Rico Libre button on his wide lapel. He spent most of his free time talking to farmers in the *campos*, trying to convince them that Muñoz Marin was not a saint. It was fortunate that his furniture business was prospering because more and more he left it to his son and his employees to run. At fourteen my brother Tato was already running the store.

"On the Island your politics can make or break your business. Papá José was lucky that he sold quality merchandise and that my brother Tato was so popular that people forgot on purpose that a *Nacionalista* owned the place. You know that Tato's store in the mall is very successful. He imports all the furniture from South America and the Orient. It's what people want now. Jorge could have managed it for him, if he had wanted to.

"Mamá María only cared about the business because it provided her with the money and the power base she needed to run her politics and her charities. I would listen to my parents talking about who needed what in the town. To this day I can hear Papá José's resigned sigh as she wrote checks for the widow left penniless, for the sick child's doctor bills, and of course for the ongoing campaigns to recruit potential voters who needed to be persuaded with food, music, and pamphlets.

"When she came into my room at night to brush my hair and hear me say my lessons for the next day, I could see that she had extraordinary energy. I also knew I was not as strong as Mamá María. And I think that she felt it too. I tried not to complain that she brushed my hair too hard; the bristles scratched my sensitive scalp. She did not mean to hurt me. And I tried to listen to her telling me stories about the brave men and women fighting to free their countries. This is what I got instead of bedtime stories. In her revolutionary tales, the women did heroic things too. But I was not interested in female soldiers; I wanted her to tell me about beautiful women falling in love with handsome princes. I wanted to see my mother dressed in flowery dresses with lace collars like other mothers instead of embarrassing me by wearing men's pants and a white cotton shirt except when she went out; then she wore black dresses and pulled her hair back in a tight bun. No lipstick either. She was a beautiful woman who could have turned heads. Instead all she wanted was to change minds and hearts. If there was a hopeless cause, Mamá María was there to lead it.

"I often studied her as she sat on my bed, this pretty woman with her tan skin and eyes as black as onyx that turned into burning coals when she was angry or excited. She looked like the Spanish/Taíno Indian woman that she was, with her high cheekbones and shiny straight black hair. She had long fingers and elegant hands. I did not inherit her beautiful hands as you can see. Mamá's voice was deep and dramatic, the voice of an actress or orator. I loved and dreaded that voice, which was always commanding, so sure in its tone. I loved it when she recited a poem from one of her books to me, although it was almost always one by the Cuban poet, Marti, whom she admired. Then she would place her cool palm on my forehead as if she were impressing the words into my head through my skin and I would fall asleep and dream dreams that she would have never approved of.

"World War II gave Mamá María all the opportunities for action that she needed. She came home one day and called me in from playing house with my dolls under the tamarind tree. She seemed excited and angry at the same time. But by this time I had learned to recognize her public emotions—she was not angry at me, but at some issue or some country, usually the United States. She sat me down on a chair facing her. And she began talking to me in a very serious tone.

" 'María Elena, hard times are coming,' my mother said. I looked at her with the attention she demanded when she talked to me in this way, although I did not know what she meant. We had always had plenty of everything. In fact, we were considered well-off by many of our poorer neighbors.

"'*Hija,* if the United States enters the war, Puerto Rican men will be going away to fight and die in this foreign conflict. It is not our war. But the men will go and die and the women will suffer. Do you understand what I am saying to you, *niña?*'

"'Will Papá José have to go and die in the war, Mamá?' I did not want this to happen even though the word *war* only meant stories of valor to me—the ones she herself told me at night.

"'No, Papá José is not a young man. They will want the young men to fight.'

"'That is good, isn't it, Mamá?' I desperately needed her to reassure me that things would always be made right, usually through her efforts.

"'No, *niña*!' Her angry voice made me jump. 'Don't be a fool! It is not good. Nothing about this war is good. But we will have to get through it. There will not be enough food for everyone. There will not be enough of anything. We will have to start organizing now.' She had forgotten about me and was pacing in her nervous way, talking as if to herself about calling a meeting of the women whose husbands and sons who would be drafted into the army. I listened, afraid of the words she was using to describe what was coming now that the world was at war. Her cheeks were flushed, and her dark eyes smoldering. I had never seen her look more beautiful or more frightening.

"Within the year, the *pueblo* changed. There were almost no young men to be seen in the baseball park or the *mercados* where they usually loitered to watch the girls. The male population was made up of older ones, sick ones, and little boys. Women were everywhere. Suddenly you saw the reclusive Doña Modesta behind the counter of her husband's grocery store, and the delicate Ramonita loading trucks at the warehouse since her brother wasn't there to do it anymore. There was Magaly at the telegraph office, and Rosa who became the postmistress. Female faces everywhere. Mamá María was in her element. She held weekly meetings at our house to find out what families were suffering the most, and in cooperation with the other women who had taken over many of the businesses, she bought food at cost and distributed it.

"Mamá María demanded a military jeep from the mayor for her work, and somehow she got it. Since Tato had to help Papá José at the store after school, I went with her on her deliveries into the countryside.

"The dirt roads were full of holes that made the jeep lurch and rear up like a wild horse, making skinny me have to hang on to the seat so that I would not end up tossed on top of someone's roof. Mamá María laughed watching my struggles. But she was a good driver, and I knew I was never in any real danger.

"The *campos* of Puerto Rico are so beautiful with their green hillsides, *verdes, verdes,* and its fruit trees perfuming the air that I actually looked forward to these mad rides to the *campesinos'* homes with my mother. The fiery orange of the Flanboyan trees in blossom is an image that was burned into my memory. There is no place more beautiful on earth.

"I did not like going into some houses, however. Sometimes there were women dressed in black sitting around looking like *fantasmas,* grieving spirits from the other world. They would accept my mother's bags of groceries and clothes in silence and offer us tepid coffee in cracked cups with no sugar or milk in it. Out of politeness we would have to drink it. I was always glad to walk out into the sunlight again. Even at noon those houses were dark.

"It was during this time, when Mamá María was busy from daybreak until late at night, that something changed between my parents. I remember hearing them argue loudly in their bedroom. From my bed I could hear the voices, but could only make out a few words. One of them was *hijos*, babies. She screamed out once *¡No mas hijos a este mundo!* No more children into this world. I thought that she was referring to the women we visited who had seven or eight little ones, all looking like little brown lizards, so small and skinny. Mamá María always commented when we left that it was irresponsible of the women to allow so many children to come into this troubled world. But why would she be yelling this out to Papá José?

"What happened next I understood only later, after I had learned about babies and blood. One day Mamá María had gone out alone and returned directly to her bed where she stayed for several days. I heard her moaning occasionally and tried to go in to her, but Papá José sent me to his sister's house in San German. I wanted to ask questions but something told me that I should not. When I came home she was pale but on her feet again. I had started bleeding that week. Once more she sat me down in front of her for a talk. She had asked me to come into the kitchen where she was making tea from some strong-smelling herbs she grew in the backyard. She poured us both a cup.

"'What is it?' I recoiled from its pungent aroma and greenish color.

"'Drink it slowly, María Elena.' She sat across from me and sipped her tea from a porcelain cup. It was always important to Mamá María to use the fine things her mother had left her. My grandmother had died in childbirth when Mamá María was already a teenager.

Women of that time had children until it killed them. As the only daughter, she had gotten the house and a little money as her inheritance. Her brothers had inherited the coffee bean farm and other land that had once belonged to her mother's family. All my life I had known that Mamá María had felt cheated of her birthright by her father, now dead also, and by her brothers—businessmen who sold the lands to developers as soon as their parents were in their graves.

"'I do not like the way it tastes.' I protested, thinking that it was a laxative she thought I needed. I had not told her about the blood, but I knew that she had seen the stains on the yellow skirt I had on when it happened. I had been in church with my aunt Alicia when I felt the sticky warm wetness between my legs. I managed to get through the mass, then I wrapped my mantilla around my waist to walk home. I did not panic when I saw the blood. Some of my friends at school had started menstruating and told the others. I was glad to have it. It meant I was a *señorita* now. Not a child anymore.

"'It helps the cramping,' she said smiling at me in a new way, as if we were two adults talking. She had also included me in when she said 'women menstruating.'

"'Now that you are a *señorita*, you must be careful, María Elena,' she said. 'You will be hearing a lot of nonsense about what the bleeding means. There are women who believe superstitions about this time of the month. You have probably heard some of these things already. Am I right?'

"'Yes,' I admitted, feeling my cheeks get hot. I hoped that Mamá María was not about to tell me in detail about sex. I also knew that if that is what she wanted to do there was nothing I could do but sit there and listen.

"She smiled again as if she had read my thoughts: 'I do not mean about having babies. I know that you have heard one fact about it at least—it takes a man and a woman to make a child. What the blood means is that your body is ready for pregnancy now. It is easy to get pregnant, Maria Elena; but difficult and painful to bring a child into this world. I will not say more about this to you now. If you want to ask me about it later . . .' To my surprise, her voice had broken into a sort of dry sob, but she composed herself quickly, took a sip from her cup, and continued: 'Do not listen to everyone who has something to warn you about. What they say will not be based on the truth but on superstition.' She went on to list some of the things that were not true about a woman's menstrual cycle that I had heard told as fact already: that you should not wash your hair during your period because you were susceptible to pneumonia and other illnesses of the chest at that time, that you should cover your head after sunset to prevent paralysis of the face, that you should avoid being in close proximity with men because they could smell your pollution and be repelled. Mamá María told me that most of these 'facts' were really old wives tales to frighten women into acting with caution around men after they got their periods. She told me that I would sometimes feel aches and pains. I should treat my symptoms with natural remedies and act as if it was all natural. She took out a white linen handkerchief from her pocket and used it to show me how I should fold the clean cloths that I would have to wear inside my underpants. 'Change them often and wash them immediately,' she said.

"I was glad our talk was over and, thanking her, I got up from my chair. Mamá María then put something else on the table. A little black box.

"'Open it,' she said.

"It was a beautiful gold chain with a medallion of the Alta Gracia Virgin on it. It looked exactly like the one she always wore on a chain around her neck until that day. I was stunned by the gift and could not think of anything to say except '*Gracias*, Mamá.'

"She took the chain from my hand and, lifting my braid, clasped it around my neck. It felt cool against my skin. The first gold jewelry I had worn.

"The Alta Gracia was my mother's patroness. When I became a woman, she gave me this chain and *medalla*. 'You know that I am not superstitious', she said, 'but I hope that this will be a reminder of the things I have told you today. Being a woman is painful: it means blood, sacrifice, and loss. But it is also a privilege. To bear a child is to perform a miracle.'

"I have never taken my chain off. Have you noticed this, *hija*?

"*Y pues*, I went from child to woman during the war. My parents worked indefatigably, but rarely together anymore. Since the day that Mamá María had come home pale and taken to her bed, they had not shared a bedroom. After a while, it seemed normal for each of them to head for different parts of the house at bedtime. The war years were prosperous for my father's business, but it required a change in his politics. It was

Mamá María's passionate objections to one of his business decisions that completed the wall of silence that went up between her and Papá José. Not that she has ever told me any of this. Never has that woman said anything about her feelings for the old man. It was not until he started getting sick in his old age that she expressed any emotion toward him. You saw him in his decline, but in those early days he was a strong, handsome man. He had a reputation as a diplomat too, and I heard people say that he could have been elected mayor of our town if he had not been a *Nacionalista*. I also heard that the women liked him. I knew of at least one who spent a lot of time at the store.

"But my parents did not argue (except once) about love. It was always about politics and Mamá María's many activities, which took her more and more away from home as we got older.

"The big explosion in our house came the day Papá José announced at the dinner table that he had accepted a contract from the Americans to sell them furniture for the base they were building in a port city south of our *pueblo*. Mamá María actually slammed her fist on the table, making the fine porcelain and crystal shake and tinkle as it hit the silverware. Papá José stared her down from his end of the table: 'María,' he said in a soft warning tone that I knew very well, 'calm yourself at this table. I tell you and the children about *this decision which I have already made* because it is for this family's benefit. You should know that we have used most of our savings in worthy causes.' He looked pointedly at her when he said this. Tato and I kept our eyes down, but I listened intently to my parents' angry confrontation. It was very unusual for them to speak so freely to each other in front of us. I normally had to eavesdrop on their discussions at night when they thought I was in bed. Papá José continued speaking in his slow, emphatic way: 'If we are to survive financially during this war, and help others as well, I will have to find new markets for our products. Our people are not buying new furniture right now. Everyone on the Island is concerned with survival, not with new beds or tables.' Mamá María continued to stare at him with a look of such fury that he finally put down his napkin and quietly left the table.

"Mamá María also got up, ordered us to finish our meal, and followed him into their bedroom. She was trembling with anger—I knew the look.

"My brother and I listened as she entered the room, slamming the door behind her. It was the first time I heard my parents shouting at each other. He called her idealistic and impractical. She called him Judas. She screamed that she would rather beg in the streets than sell her soul to imperialists. Then suddenly a name I recognized was shouted out by Papá José. It was the name of a poet whose work Mamá María had read to me at bedtime long ago. He was famous for having died a martyr to the cause for independence, gunned down in Nueva York where he had gone to raise money for the *Revolución*. What Papá José had shouted to Mamá María was: 'You should have gone with the other radical students to Nueva York. You would have been happy there with your sophisticated friends. You have never been happy being merely the wife of a shopkeeper!'

"There was silence then, the slammed door we heard after that was our father leaving the house. We did not see him again for two days. Mamá María acted strangely the two nights that he was away. She spent the night sitting in her rocker on the dark porch. I know because I listened to the rhythmic sound it made until I fell asleep.

"I think of those years when our town lost so many of its young men in battlefields and oceans far away from home, but what I remember best are the women; their haunted eyes as they lined up outside the telegraph office to read the lists in alphabetical order to see if their men were listed. The lists were done according to the American's idea of last names, so that time after time there was anguish and relief as women came across what they thought was a son's or husband's name only to discover that it was someone else listed by his maternal surname, which everyone carries as a second last name in Puerto Rico. The confusion resulted in many men being listed incorrectly as dead or missing in action, and later, veterans, widows, and orphans having many problems proving their identities to receive benefits. The picture I have in my head is of women descending into the town like skinny blackbirds, a trail of ragged children in tow. Mamá María and I were usually there during the postings of the lists so that we could dispense bags of food and medicines to women who lived so far into the country that we could not find them, they had to find us. I avoided looking into those ravaged faces as I handed the packages out. There were few words exchanged since charity is not something people discuss. You could see how ashamed it made some of them to take the food, but the children stared at the bags with such famished eyes that they reminded me of the starved cats and dogs you sometimes saw at the edges of roads waiting for a crumb to fall.

"I knew this for a fact: What my mother was doing separated her from the community. She could not be friends with the women she helped. They would not let her come any closer than the arm's length she extended to hand them the bags of food. How can you sit down and talk naturally with someone from whom you have accepted charity? We both understood this and worked in silence. No chitchat or gossip like there would have been in better times, when they would have still been poorer than us, but not downtrodden charity cases.

"I knew that my mother was lonely. The other women in our town who could have been her friends—the wives of the banker, the lawyer, the government employees; other educated, middle-class people—she found boring, and they returned her disdain by keeping her outside their dress-up circles of benefit dinners and social events. I could see from my viewpoint as a lonely child that Mamá María had an aura of energy around her that frightened people away. Even me. I had to pretend to be sick sometimes to get relief from her demanding pace. I was a daydreamer all of my life. The one doll I was allowed to have only at Papá José's insistence became my fantasy daughter, my spoiled child. I dressed her in feminine clothes that I made from scraps and showed her off to my imaginary friends—and my imaginary husband, a beautiful young man who treated me like a princess.

"I pretended to have a headache one day and played with my doll in my room—although I was already past the age for dolls and a *señorita* as well. Mamá María had stayed home that evening. I knew that she was exhausted. She was lying down on a hammock when a loud knock came at the front door, although it was open—nobody locked their front door back then—except to go to bed or if there had been a death or tragedy in the family. I came out of my room to see who it was. In the shadows of our porch there stood an old woman, her head covered with a black shawl. My mother seemed to know her and stepped out to greet her. From what I could make out, this woman was a midwife. She had come to ask my mother for assistance in a difficult delivery. It was not until then that I knew that my mother also had had training in delivering babies. I saw her go into her room and get her large first-aid bag that she often took into the houses of women with sick children, to teach them how to care for their minor illnesses and injuries.

"She saw me standing in the doorway to my bedroom. I still had my doll in my arms: 'Would you like to come with me, María Elena? I am going to help Doña Anita bring a baby into the world. It is a breech birth—coming out feet-first, and we must hurry.' She looked at the doll in my arms and she smiled. 'You can bring your baby-doll along. Come.'

"Had I heard sarcasm in her voice that night? Pain? I was too inexperienced to tell then. The house we went into that night was my father's mistress's *casa*. It was the house he had set up with his *querida* sometime after the day Mamá María had come home pale and sick and taken to her bed for days. I did not know it then. But after my half sister was born, it became an open secret in our *pueblo*. Of course, my mother never talked about it, although everyone knew that if she had not been there helping Doña Anita pull that big girl out of her screaming mother, neither one of them would have made it through the night.

"This is what I saw when I went into the house with Mamá María: a small home completely furnished from my father's store. I recognized each item, could have told you how much it cost. It was his very best merchandise: cedar and mahogany pieces handmade on the Island by craftsmen contracted by Don José himself. These days they are worth a fortune. My mother scanned the room quickly with her eyes, but did not say anything. She followed the screams to the bedroom. There on a tall poster bed was a woman we both knew by sight, a divorcee who had recently moved to our *pueblo* from another town. She looked possessed. Blood was dripping from her lip where she had bitten it. She was so taken over by her pain that she grabbed me by my leg screaming for help. It took my mother and Doña Anita both to pry her fingers away. It frightened me so much that I started to run out of the room, but my mother said *no*. I was to sit just outside the door to the room and listen for her instructions.

"I never forgot that night: the scream that went on without a breath piercing my ears and making me feel like I was suffocating; the warm, sweet smell of blood that the old woman brought out of the room in pans making a thin red trail into the kitchen. Mamá María would say in a calm tone, 'María Elena, bring me towels from the wardrobe in the hallway,' or bring me scissors which you will find in such and such a place. I did what she told me and never questioned how she knew where these things were. Later I understood that she was aware that this was Papá José's house too, and he was an obsessively organized man.

"I must have finally fallen asleep toward dawn because the last thing I remember was hearing a baby cry, then being lifted up onto my feet by Mamá María. I started to cry out when I saw how her white shirt was soaked with blood, but she placed her hand gently over my mouth, shaking her head to let me know that she was all right, that it was not her blood. I must have been very tired because I left my doll in that house. I never went back for her either. That night I learned how much blood there is in a woman, and how much it takes to have a child. I discovered just how strong my mother was, that she could bring her own husband's baby out of another woman's body with her own hands, and how, practically drained of life herself, she could lift me up out of my last dream of childhood and take me home, the only place that I have felt safe in all of my life. That night I outgrew dolls and began to understand what drove my mother.

"It was love. She believed in love, although not always in romance. By the time I was fifteen, I had been my mother's assistant for many years. I had distributed food and clothes during the war years, I had helped her tend to the sick women and children, I had drawn charts of parts of the human body on our portable chalkboard to teach basic hygiene and birth control to girls not much older than me already carrying swollen bellies around. I did what she told me, but I dreamed of the day when the curfews and bomb drills would be over and I could replace my rubber boots with satin slippers. I know you probably think that I'm a hopeless romantic, but how can you know how years of walking in mud and talking only of sickness, hunger, and war can make a young girl yearn for someone special to come along and take her away.

"The most romantic thing I ever saw my mother do was to help the dying lovers. One day Mamá María and I were walking, or rather slipping, down a muddy embankment toward our jeep. We had left it by the side of the little stone bridge because we were afraid it would get stuck if we tried to drive it up to the house we were visiting that day. It was almost dark and we were holding on to each other's waists to keep our balance. Halfway down, Mamá María stopped abruptly; I slipped down into the mud, almost pulling her down.

"'Listen,' she said, helping me back up. I did not hear anything, concerned only with the awful smell and feel of mud on my clothes and hair. I just wanted to get home and take a bath. We stood in the twilight listening for a few minutes.

"'Look at the jeep,' Mamá said in a whisper. Then I saw the reflection of the flickering light on the windshield of our vehicle. The source was obviously a small fire under the bridge. I became frightened thinking it was an escaped convict hiding out. Every day we read in the paper of the exploits of one man who was moving around the Island, just ahead of the authorities. Women hid him out, they said, because he was so handsome and charming. The newspapers claimed that he was dangerous, although his crime had been to kill the man who had raped his wife. The murdered man was the son of a politician who was now obsessed with hunting down his son's assassin. It was like a *novela* in daily installments, a story like the radio dramas most women, with the exception of Mamá María, were addicted to in our *pueblo*. I also listened to these *novelas* on my own radio Papá José had given me, and I read the newspapers after Mamá discarded them. I confess to have been fascinated by the handsome convict, but that night we spotted the campfire under the bridge, I was simply terrified. But not my mother.

"She must have known that no smart escaped convict would hide so near a road with a car nearby. She gave me the keys to the jeep, which I could already drive, and told me to sit behind the wheel and crank the engine. She was going to investigate. Heart pounding, wet and miserable, I followed her back to the bridge. I aimed the jeep's headlights into the cavernous interior as she had instructed. From within we both heard gasps, as if someone had been startled or hurt by the light.

"'Wait here,' Mamá said. I watched her walk through the arch made by the bridge but could not see beyond the entrance where she disappeared. Hands clutching the steering wheel, I asked myself whether I would have the courage to go in after her if I heard her scream or if she did not come out. I prayed intensely that this would not happen. I have always known that I am not the adventurous woman that she is.

"I did not have to wait too long before she came out again.

"'Get me the blankets and my bag, María Elena,' she said from the mouth of the cave, then she went back in. I did as she told me, grabbing the army blankets and the medical kit that Mamá María always kept in the back of the jeep.

"Carefully, leaving the engine running and the lights on, I made my way into the low cave under the bridge. I was shocked by what I saw there.

"In front of a tiny fire made from sticks and twigs, two deathly pale people lay wrapped in a thin sheet that made them look like shrouded corpses. One of them, a young man, was on his elbows. The other was a girl with long black hair fanned around a cadaverous yet beautiful face. Her eyes were closed. Above the sheet, their hands were clasped tightly. The boy and my mother were talking, although he kept his eyes on the girl sleeping next to him.

"'María Elena, this is Francisco. Her name is Amapola. You stay where you are, just hand me the blankets.'

"Amapola, the tropical hibiscus. One of the most beautiful of Puerto Rico's flowers. I used to put one in my hair sometimes because I liked to see the contrast of the scarlet flower set against my black hair. But its blossom wilts rapidly. The petals feel almost like skin, but they are so delicate that they almost melt in your fingers. I looked at the girl. There were deep red spots on her cheeks, but she looked feverish, not healthy. I stood at the wall and watched my mother wrap the rough green blankets around the couple. The girl's eyelids flickered and her lips moved as if to speak, but she was too weak. Francisco tucked the blanket around her lovingly, although he too sank down unable to hold his head up any longer. My mother took several bottles from her bag and put them next to him.

"'Aspirins, alcohol, cough syrup. It is all I have. But I will come back tonight with hot coffee and food.' Getting no response from the boy, who seemed to have either fainted or fallen asleep, Mamá María got on her knees next to him and felt his forehead. She took off the cape she was wearing and gently eased it under their heads, which had been resting on the cold, wet cobblestones.

"Before we left, we gathered what little dry kindling we could find and she added it to their pathetic little fire. On the way home she told me what she knew about Francisco and Amapola.

"'They are from *el asilo.* I have shown you the hospital where tuberculosis patients live. It is deep in the country, near here. No one wants these sick people around. And, María Elena, I have never asked you to keep anything from your father, but you must not tell him what you saw tonight. He would be furious that I exposed you to this illness . . . and myself. You have to promise me that you will not tell anyone.'

"'Will someone come and get them, Mamá? We have to tell the police that they have escaped from the *asilo.*' I was afraid that we were breaking some law, especially since Mamá María did not want Papá José to know. I had feared her being arrested again since the Ponce incident.

"'María Elena, Francisco and Amapola are not escaped prisoners. That is, they are treated as if they were criminals because they have tuberculosis. They are ordinary people, just like you and me. But they are dying. That is the main difference. Francisco told me that he has been in the hospital since he was fifteen. He is now eighteen. He met Amapola there when she was brought in this year. She is also eighteen. They are in love.'

"'They will die under the bridge, Mamá. Don't they need medicines? Wouldn't they rather be in their own beds than on the ground?' The lovers' predicament had really touched me; but in my wet, muddy clothes I could not imagine choosing to be out on a night like this, sick and hungry under an embankment.

"'In the hospital they are kept apart. They can only see each other for minutes each day. You have to understand, María Elena, that both of these young people are very ill. They do not have long to live. Francisco told me that Amapola's condition is particularly serious. He heard a nurse say that it was a matter of days for her. They found ways of exchanging notes by passing them from patient to patient. Many of the other friends they have in the hospital helped them to leave tonight. They want to be together for a little while. He was afraid that we were the police when he heard us, but he prayed that the jeep belonged to me. They just could not go any further.' My mother reached for my hand in the darkness, 'They know of my work, María Elena, they talk about it in the hospital.' She seemed so pleased, I hesitated to ask any more questions. But although I too was on the side of the lovers, it seemed to me that it was wrong to not tell their doctors, or at least the priest. If they died under the bridge, would it be our fault?

"'Are you sending the ambulance for them, Mamá?'

"'No. I cannot break my promise to Francisco. There is nothing more doctors can do for those two. Tonight I will return to the bridge and take them the food and clothes I promised Francisco. You will stay home, and if your father comes home to sleep, you will tell him that I have been called away on an emergency.'

"It was only half of a lie. It shamed me to know where Papá José would be spending the night if he did not come home. I had seen the woman with her baby daughter once in town. The girl resembled me in my baby pictures. That made sense because I strongly favored him.

"'I am doing the right thing, María Elena. Please trust me.' My mother said this with humility in her voice, as if she were talking to another woman, an equal, who would understand that sometimes love must take precedence over logic.

"'I do trust you,' I said.

"That night, in my comfortable bed I stayed awake waiting for her to return from the lovers' cave. I imagined them holding each other close all through the rainy night, and I thought: How lucky they are.

"Seeing the dying lovers had awakened something in me. When Mamá María showed me the lurid picture in the paper of the two thin bodies wrapped in sheets being loaded onto a flatbed truck by men in masks and gloves I cried so hard that I surprised her into tears too. But I was weeping not just out of sadness for them—my grief came from a source I had just discovered, a yearning to love and to be loved by a man. My skin was hungry for a touch I had not experienced before. For the first time in my life I felt naked under my clothes. It was a hunger of the flesh and of the spirit that I could not satisfy with anything in my life then."

My mother paused in her story, apparently embarrassed that she had told me such intimate details about her feelings. Her voice was different when she began talking again. It was as if she had forgotten that it was me there. She was traveling back in time. I was far away in her future. Would she bring her story all the way forward toward me? She looked down into her cup as if she were seeing things in the black coffee that were too painful to speak.

Her voice was soft when she continued: "You know, *hija*, you gave my life a center. Having a baby almost made me forget how much I missed my mother and my island. Every day I would go stand by your crib while you slept. I couldn't believe you were my own little girl.

"Taking care of you helped me to lose myself; I was too tired to be homesick or to have dreams of my own; Jorge busied himself more and more with his job and his barrio life. I saw how you grew away from me, and I began to be lonely again. As soon as you could walk and talk I knew that you would not be like him or me; from the start, you were a willful child and wise beyond your years. Although I spoke only in Spanish to you,

you learned English from the TV, talking back to the characters and demanding in tears that I take you to where they lived, in those beautiful houses on tree-lined streets. Jorge bought you those little books at the grocery store, do you remember them? He taught you to read *Bambi* when you were four years old. You always preferred playing teacher than playing with dolls. I was glad that you showed so much independence, but frankly, it bothered me that you never took much interest in dressing up in the fancy clothes I bought you, or in shopping for that matter. Once again I lost my chance to play at dolls.

"Still, you were a comfort to me in your own way. Once you learned how to read English quite well, you would translate recipes from boxes of cereal to make treats that you saw advertised on TV. You would read a word, and if you did not know it in Spanish, we would look it up in the dictionary, and I would cook with the picture in front of me because it had to look just right. Sometimes you would ask me to tell you about my mother and father in Puerto Rico and I would take out my photo album and tell your stories about my childhood there. Do you remember? You particularly liked to hear me tell about Mamá María. I always made my mother a strong heroine in my stories, and I told you a fairy-tale version of how your father and I met. Your favorite one was of how we found the lovers under the bridge. The same one I told you today, but I made it a fairy tale. You always asked me a dozen questions about it.

"'How old were they?' you always wanted to know.

"'Eighteen.'

"'Tell me again why they were sick.'

"'Tuberculosis is an illness of the chest—the lungs, *hija*. They coughed a lot and they had a fever.'

"'Like when you give me medicine and feel my head to see if it's hot?'

"'Much more serious than when you have a cold.'

"'Did they die?'

"'Yes.'

"'Will I die?'

"'Not for a very long time. Let's not talk about death.' I always had to end our story-telling time when you got stuck on a subject. 'Let's check these things in the oven.'

"'They are called brownies, Mother. *When* will I die?'

"'They look ready to me. Let's try one.'

"'We have to wait until they cool. It says so on the box. Will I die if I get tuber . . . what you said the boy and the girl had?'

"'You're not going to get tuberculosis, Elenita. They have medicines for it now. I am not going to answer any more silly questions about dying!'

"'Will you tell me another story?'

"If I had not loved you so much you would have driven me crazy. You were like a sponge soaking up everything that you heard or saw, and by the time you started school, I was eager for a few hours without the bombardment of your questions. I was more nervous than you were about going to school that first day, and I cried, but you didn't, when I saw you disappear into the huge red-brick building. I was there an hour early, waiting outside the door at the end of your first school day. You came out smiling, carrying a notebook and a pencil.

"'It's so easy. They're doing baby work,' you told me, showing me the notebook with lines an inch apart and samples of letters. 'I know all my letters and how to sound words out, so the teacher told me I could be her helper.'"

She touched my hand tentatively.

"Do you remember, *hija*?"

I did and didn't remember what she described. She had spotlighted all the good parts. But she was right about one thing: I am different from my parents. And yet now that he was gone, I missed my father too. I wanted my mother to keep talking and fill in the blanks so that I could find my place in their story.

"Mami, you were telling me about the year you turned fifteen."

"Ah, *sí, sí*. When they turned fifteen, other girls of our town got their *quinceañera* parties. But my mother thought these debuts were disgraceful—mere spectacles for the girls' parents to show off their daughters and their wealth. It was true that small fortunes were spent on these affairs. The girls were treated like beauty queens in their formal gowns and accompanied by attendants and escorts. The town's dance hall was usually rented and a band hired to play. We could have afforded it, my father would have gladly allowed it, but Mamá did not even ask me. She informed me that the money we would have spent on *espectaculos* would be put away in the bank for me. I have yet to see that money. As a birthday gift, she gave me five dollars to spend on myself, in any way I liked. Five dollars was not just loose change then, and I saw the effort it cost her to say the words: Mamá María liked to be in control at all times, but it was my fifteenth birthday.

"The previous week, Mamá had taken me shopping for new shoes, black patent leather pumps and cloth for dresses—the patterns she would choose had darts at the bodice to accommodate my new figure.

"We had taken the train to the nearby *pueblo* of San German, where her favorite seamstress lived. When the train pulled up, the conductor, a red-faced man, had blown the whistle while waving at me. This annoyed Mamá María, but as the breeze raised by the train's braking caught and lifted my skirt above my knees, I felt like a movie actress—like the Mexican movie star, María Felix.

"There is no feeling comparable to walking in the sun in Puerto Rico. During the darkest winters of my exile I have remembered days like that one when I was fifteen, at the peak of my youth, shopping in the ancient town of hills and cobblestone streets. Everyone seemed to know Doña María. We stopped at every other store so that she could exchange news of her party with people. But I noticed that, although her fervor was respected, most people wanted to talk about the new party in power led by the poet turned politician, Luis Muñoz Marin, an eloquent senator who was leading the Island in an inspired race out of the struggle of the war years. His catchy motto, *Jalda, arriba!*—onward, upward!—could be heard shouted out by children in school yards, returning GIs getting off their ships at San Juan harbor, and by just about everyone caught in the spirit of the time. Mamá María was not as convinced as the others about Muñoz

Marin, *El Vate*, as he was affectionately called, the bard. As the son of the great statesman, Muñoz Rivera, he was expected to fight for the Island's autonomy, but Mamá María claimed that Muñoz was already talking more like a poet than a revolutionary. Yet I had seen his power revealed: people wept with emotion at the beauty of his words when he described the Island and its destiny. On my Island, everyone loves poetry, we carry it in our blood—this need to make beautiful words hang together like a pearl necklace.

"That day in San German I felt proud of being seen with Doña María. She took the long way to the seam-stress's house, up the hill toward Porta Coeli, one of the oldest churches on the Island. I could tell she too felt good walking in the sun. She crossed herself as we passed the church, out of habit, since she only went to mass now when someone got married or died. But she did point out its Spanish-style architecture, and we stopped to eat a coconut ice-cream cone on its steps. From there we could see the houses built at a slant on the hills, and at the bottom, the town circling the plaza with its cement benches and shade trees. We watched the Catholic schoolgirls from el Colegio San José being led by nuns to the church. They looked like little ducks dressed in their heavily starched white uniforms following the winged coifs of the sisters' habits, in sin-gle file. Mamá María winked at me, as amused as I was by the sight. This shopping trip was like no other in my childhood. It marked the beginning of a brief inter-lude before I married when Mamá María treated me like an adult most of the time and when I began to appreciate her energy and her drive. The whole Island seemed to be rising from its sickbed after the war. Young men were returning from the army, marrying, starting families. The new government led by the poet was ours for the time being—although we had the American Governor Tugwell in office—there was hope for self-rule eventually. It was *jalda, arriba!*—the feeling was contagious, a perfect atmosphere to be fifteen years old, to be in love with love.

"So I decided to take a peek at my future. One day I went over to my friend Magda's house and convinced her to go with me to Madama's house in the country. We told her parents that we were going to the matinee in town so they would not expect us home too soon: it was an hour's walk into the country to the palm reader's house. I was feeling excited that day. It was not just an ordinary prediction I was expecting. For a long time I had felt that I was waiting for something big to happen in my life. My body had changed completely in one year. I had gone from being a skinny child to a woman with breasts and hips. And most amazing of all to me, I was now able to look Mamá María in the eyes.

"And so in my new dress and high-heeled shoes I started out with Magda toward Madama's house in the country. It was a stupid thing to do, since after leaving the town the road was all dirt and rocks. My feet hurt as if I were walking on nails and coals. Finally I asked Magda to stop. We were at the artesian well where people had once drawn their water from Taíno Indian times. Some of the country people still used it. The smooth, wet stepping stones felt wonderful under my feet after I took off my shoes and put them away in my pocketbook. I felt foolish doing that, but we were still a half hour away from the palm reader's house. I knew I could not make it with shoes on my tortured feet. Magda and I sat on a large rock worn into a sort of park bench by hundreds of years of use. We listened to the song of the *coqui* in the thick foliage beyond the well. The thumb-size tree frog usually sings its two-note song at night, or after a rain, but in this little grove, it found the moisture and shade it needed for inspiration. Magda broke the silence with a shocking revelation. I have noticed in my life that secluded places such as forests and caves make a person want to reveal their secrets. Why is that so? Perhaps it just happens to Catholics who are accustomed to confessing their sins in a dark little closet. If I have a secret, I stay away from such places unless I am alone.

"What Magda said was: 'I am not a virgin anymore, María Elena.'

"I nearly fell into the well at my feet. Magda and I were the same age, fifteen. We were as close as sisters and she had never told me she had a *novio*. In our town when a girl started to see a boy, an engagement announcement soon followed. It was almost impossible for a girl to see a boy alone. I waited for her to speak. This was a big thing. Would she have a baby now? Magda looked back at me from her seat on another big rock. She started sobbing into her hands. I went over and embraced her.

"'He forced me to do it. I am so ashamed. No one will ever want to marry me, ever.' Magda's words confused me. She had not made love with a man she loved, this was obvious. Who could it be?

"She soon told me: 'It was Señor Ruiz, the history teacher.'

"'I do not believe it. He is our *maestro*.'

"'He is also a man. An evil man who tricked me. You remember that he sent a note to my parents asking them to allow me to stay after school for tutoring. He had given me low grades in my tests this year.'

"'We studied together for them. We knew the lessons by heart,' I said. I was trying to imagine the history teacher embracing Magda. The thought of that old man—he was in his thirties, at least twice as old as we—attacking my friend made me sick.

"'He was doing it on purpose. Giving me those bad grades so that he would have a reason to make me stay after school.'

"'What did he do to you. Did he hurt you?' I wanted to tell Mamá María and get the man fired from his job. But I was not entirely naive even then. Magda would be publicly shamed, too.

"'At first he pretended just to be concerned about me. He put his hand on my arm, then he would move it down to my waist. It all happened so slowly that I could not find words to complain. He is a teacher! What could I say, do not touch my arm? Then one day he took me to the back of the room, where there is a storage area for maps and books. He said he wanted me to help him find a book we needed. When we went in he forced me down on the floor . . .'

"Magda broke down completely then. She cried aloud like a heartbroken child. In that quiet place her cries echoed, and the *coquí* stopped singing. I comforted her as best I could, stroking her head and telling her that I was her sister. After she calmed down a little, she described what I now know was a rape. She said: *me hizo el mal.* Those are misleading words, a soft way of saying the unspeakable truth about a woman who is violated, changed, damaged by a man. It does not sound like the horrible thing it is.

"Magda and I held hands and talked for a long time, promising each other to not tell anyone our secrets, ever. I have kept my promise to her although she has been dead for thirty years. She died giving birth to the baby of a man she loved and married.

"That day on our way to hear our future's predicted, we did not know that love can both heal and destroy. We were just hurrying to meet our destiny, which our bodies were telling us would arrive in the shape of a lover. At fifteen, a person is still half child and as we walked through the flowering trees to Madama's little house we started to forget what had happened to Magda and soon we were talking about a party we had not been to and even to laugh a little. From the distance of my years now I am amazed at how easily pain can be absorbed by a young mind— the impulse is to fly and it takes a heavy stone chained to your neck to keep you on the ground. *Asi es la vida.*

"We saw Madama hanging her laundry on a line tied from two palm trees as we approached the little clearing of her property. She was small and slender like a little girl. Her skin was so black that in the direct sunlight it looked cobalt blue, and her face had so many wrinkles—from working in the fields her entire life— that it was hard to find her deep-set eyes. She always wore a bright red bandanna on her head and a long black dress with buttons, dozens of them, from her neck to her ankles. Madama looked like the sacred doll that *santeros* use in their rites—a goddess from Africa called *La Madama*—and that is where she had gotten her nickname. Her real name was Monina and she had been a slave as a young girl.

"She was nearly one hundred years old now, or so they said, and a *partera*, a midwife to the country women who were afraid of male doctors and hospitals. Many of the children she had delivered and in many cases cared for during their mother's illnesses or early deaths called her Mamá Monina. Mamá María spoke of her with respect except on the matter of her palm reading, which she denounced as dangerous superstition.

"Madama saw us coming and rushed to hug us. She treated everyone as her own child. Although her head only came to my chin, I felt the incredible strength of her arms. They say that Madama used to cut sugar cane along with the men, and haul it in bundles on her back to the mill. She gave us her blessing: *Dios las bendiga, hijas.* And we answered *Amen.*

"Although she talked casually to both of us, asking us about our parents and about school, Madama kept staring at Magda. Then as we were sitting at her table with cups of *cafe negro* in front of us, Madama said to Magda: 'You must unburden your heart, daughter. Do not be afraid to tell me what has wounded you so deeply that it has left lines on your brow.'

"Magda broke down again. She fell on her knees and buried her face in the old woman's lap. After she had heard the story of the teacher who had violated Magda, Madama helped her back onto the chair.

"'You will not tell your parents?'

"'I can't.' Magda looked terrified at the suggestion. 'My father would not believe me. He might even send me away. He is always threatening to send me to the mountain *pueblo* where his mother lives. My mother always obeys him.'

"'Are you pregnant?' Madama continued to look intently into Magda's eyes, crunching up her face like a sponge.

"Magda shook her head: 'I bled this month.'

"'Can you keep him away from you, *niña*?'

"'I have to run home after school every day. I think that he will not dare to pursue me. He is interested in another girl now.'

"Madama nodded: 'Do you feel that you are ruined, Magda? Do you wonder whether any man will want to marry you now?'

"Magda nodded, the tears running down her face.

"'Then remember this: the man who loves you will not care that a beast injured you once. Consider what this evil man did to you as the bite of a wild animal. The scars will heal and the poison will leave your body. Today I will give you some herbs to boil and pour into your bath. They are from plants that I grow myself to heal the wounds of women. Will you do as I say?'

"In answer Magda embraced the old woman. Madama kissed her on the forehead and then turned to me: 'You are waiting for a prediction of love? *¿Si?* It will cost you one peso.'"

My mother laughed remembering the old fortune-teller. For a few moments I thought that she would leave the story right there, but I wanted the story to be complete.

"So what did Madama predict about your prince?"

"The first thing Madama revealed to me about your father was that he was from another town and would not arrive in our *pueblo* to claim me for several more years. That is how it was. He came from Ponce, a big city even back then. His family moved to our town because his father got a job with the government, the United States government, to build roads. But that wasn't until I was seventeen and had heard Madama tell me a little more about your father every year: she knew that his destiny—our destiny—would be to travel far away from the Island, and that there would be trouble between our families. That is what happened. But I was prepared for it. I knew I would marry your father the minute I saw him at the political rally.

"After the war Mamá María had to give up a lot of her activities. That really upset her—to see her husband going off to argue and fight for their beliefs while she stayed at home taking care of us. Anyway, the *Nacionalistas* wanted the Island to break away from the U.S. They still do. Mamá sends me their newspaper occasionally, but it's not the same. Before the war they were opposed to anything American taking root on the Island.

"It so happened that I met your father the night that the *Nacionalistas*, my mother among them, marched up to the town hall to protest the building of roads to transport American soldiers around the

Island. The man in charge of that project was your father's father. There they stood father and son facing mother and daughter. Because Mamá María had dragged my brother and me to the meeting against Papa's wishes.

"Well, they shouted horrible things at each other for a long time. She was called anti-progressive, and she called them lackeys for the imperialists. But I don't remember much about their insults because I was looking at your father and he was looking back. The next day he sent me a love letter at school via my friend. He had cut a picture of himself into a heart shape and pasted it to the paper. He asked me to meet him after school. That is how it began.

"That day your Papa and I talked while Magda kept a lookout. If my father were to see me talking to any boy on the street, and this boy in particular, I would have gotten punished. My parents were not the kind to beat their children, but they came up with very effective punishments nevertheless; with me it was keeping me from going to school. In those days there were no laws about children having to go to school. If the parents wanted or needed them at home, they just did it. Especially with girls. Most of them quit school at fourteen or fifteen to get engaged or married anyway. But my mother wanted me to get an education. When she made me stay at home, she would get the assignments from my teachers and I had to do the work anyway. The punishment for me was the social part of it, you see. I hated being cooped up in the house. School was my social life. The rest of the time I went to political functions with my mother and to school activities that were heavily chaperoned of course. So I had to be careful about talking with your father, although I felt in my heart that I was not doing anything wrong. After only a few meetings Jorge asked me right out; 'María Elena Fuentes, will you be my sweetheart?' And he presented me with a Spanish/English dictionary.

"'What is this for?' I opened the thick book and found a rose pressed in it. I was nervous, keeping an eye on Magda, who was sitting on a cement bench that faced the street keeping watch for my father. Jorge and I were behind the first-grade classroom where we could see her.

"'When I graduate from high school in June, I am going to Nueva York. I am hoping you will be with me.'

"I was not really surprised that he was saying these things on our first conversation. Our eyes had met at the town hall, remember? And I had known that something like this would happen in my life from what Madama had been reading on my palm for years. Still, my head was spinning a little as I listened to Jorge telling me of his plans to open a business in the States. His father was encouraging him by writing to his contacts there and with a promise to give him a certain amount of cash money when he graduated. I think I giggled and turned red because as a sort of joke, every few sentences he would say, 'Will you marry me, María Elena Fuentes, will you marry me?'

"'Not if I have to pass a test in English first,' I finally answered him.

"Suddenly he turned serious. 'I will teach you English, María Elena, and everything else you will need to know for our life together.'

"I saw then that he was very determined in his plans. I filled my head and my heart with his visions of a life where he and I would be our own masters in a place where everyone had a fair chance at success. I told him about my parents dislike of his father, how the night of the confrontation at the town hall, Mamá María had come home furious about *Los Americanos* and the Puerto Ricans who had sold out to them changing the face of the Island to make it one giant military base. She believed that the roads Jorge's father was building were not for the good of the people, but to move military trucks and make it easy to bring in more and more soldiers. Jorge told me that the same thing had happened at his house where his father had called my mother a throwback to colonial times, afraid of progress. We realized then that we were in for a struggle with our families. But for the first time in my life the thought of facing my mother did not make me weak, it had the opposite effect: as I looked at Jorge's determined face, I saw myself standing next to him, like in a formal picture, like the one we had done for our last anniversary together, and I knew that I belonged with him. I wanted to tell my parents right away, but Jorge advised me to wait until it was almost time for his graduation, so that I would not be taken out of school.

"You see how it all happened just as I knew it would? Jorge and I saw each other secretly for months after that. Magda, the girl in my wedding photo, she was my maid of honor, helped us by being our lookout and our messenger. When Jorge and I ran into each other at our parents' political meetings, we did not speak, of course, but the looks we exchanged! We spoke volumes, it was poetry! Finally, in May, Jorge came to our door one evening. I stayed in my room, as we had planned, while he talked to my father on the porch. The voices got louder and louder. Mamá María came in and found me crying from nerves. I will never forget her face. For what seemed an eternity she just looked at me with those eyes of hers, with that cold gaze that I have seen men cower under. She just stood there and waited for me to say something, or to break down.

"'I am marrying Jorge, Mamá. You cannot stop me.'

"'You are a fool, María Elena. If you were as smart as I thought you were, you would make something of yourself instead of believing the lies of the first man who looks at you.' Her words were drenched in vinegar. She had never looked at me with so much disdain. But she was not finished yet; she chose that day to tell me about plans she had for me, plans that I would now have to reject.

"'I have been saving my money for your future. I had not told you because I was waiting to see whether you deserved my sacrifice. The money I inherited from my mother, I put away for your education. You have been such a good student, and you have shown love for your studies—that is why I chose to punish you by keeping you home from school. I was testing you! This year I was going to show you what I had planned.' Mamá María then pulled an envelope from her skirt's pocket. It was a letter from the director of a teachers' college in San Juan advising my mother on how to enroll me at the school in a year's time. That is when I broke down and cried. She misunderstood my tears and took me in her arms. There I found the strength I needed to push her gently away. 'I am so sorry, Mamá. But my destiny is to marry Jorge Cordero.'

"Then she pushed *me* away, not so gently, and without saying a word left the room. I heard her calling Papa in from the porch. From my window I watched Jorge walking away. He looked back at the house once and a ray of sun caught the rim of his gold frame glasses. I will never forget how the light fell on the tears running down his face. We were no more than children really. Now I understand that Mamá was trying to protect me."

My mother paused at this point in the story. So while she poured us another cup of coffee, I asked her for the first time, "Have you ever wondered how your life would have been if you had gone to that teachers' college, Mami?"

"In times when your father and I were having troubles, one of us would bring it up. I would say, If I had taken my mother's advice, I would not be in this situation. Or he would say, 'If you had done what your mother wanted, you would not be stuck here with me.' So you see, we used my mother's offer as a weapon to hurt each other. But I have always known that I could not trade your father's love for anything else.'

"That's very sweet, Mother, but did you ever think of going back to school after you were married?"

"*Hija.*" My mother's voice took on a resigned tone when she said things to me that she felt were redundant, given what we knew about each other. "Those were different times. Ours was an old-fashioned marriage. I stayed home and took care of you, and when he needed my help at the restaurant, I did what I could there. You know how proud your father was. It would have hurt him if I had gone outside the home to work."

"You could have made your own money and bought that house you always wanted."

"And now I will tell you about our wedding." My mother does not believe that smooth transitions are always necessary. If she does not want to discuss something, she simply lumps out of one topic into another. If I were to object, she would justify it by informing me that I had interrupted her story. And she would be technically correct. I settle back with my strong cup of *café con leche.*

At least the tears have stopped momentarily as she time travels to find my father and herself as a young couple, feeling invincible in their love.

"In the months that followed Mamá María stopped talking to me almost completely. She went to the high school, and told them that I would not be returning since I was now engaged. That hurt me a lot since I then had no way of seeing Jorge. That is when we decided to elope. But his father found out about our plans and came to see Papa. I eavesdropped from the kitchen. The two men were angry but they agreed that it was better if Jorge finished school and we got married in the church since it was obvious that they could not dissuade us. I remember how my head swam from pure joy when I heard them say this.

"That night Mamá María came into my room with a huge box. In it was her beautiful wedding gown and veil. Without wasting words she told me to try it on. It fit almost perfectly, except for the bosom, which needed taking in. After pinning it, she put it back in the box. Then she gave me a notebook.

"'Here is a list of things you will need to do before your *bodas*. The way she said wedding let me know now that she was still very angry but determined that things would be done right—that is, done her way. 'You may add names of people that you want to invite. Keep the list short. I intend for this wedding to be a small affair and over with as quickly as possible.' These were the most words she had spoken to me since Jorge had talked to my father. I just kept saying, "*Sí, Mamá*" to everything she said. After all, I had expected even more trouble than I had gotten. But, as always, Mamá María knew just the right kind of punishment to inflict on me: silence and isolation from my family and my school friends. It just about killed me. Even my brother, who had been away at business school in San Juan, had come home and ignored me too.

"Before leaving with her box Mamá María asked me, 'Where do you and your future husband intend to live after the wedding?' This was her way of telling me that we could not live with her. The usual thing would have been for the new couple to live for a while at the home of in-laws or parents. Sometimes in Puerto Rico, one or more of the grandchildren are born in the grandparents' home. Young people were not in a hurry to be on their own like they are now. But Jorge had already made it clear to me that we would be leaving the Island.

"'Nueva York.' I could hardly get my mouth to say the two words. I couldn't tell her that I really didn't know exactly where we were going. Jorge was not specific about it. I don't think he had a clear idea either. All of the United States were Nueva York to us in those days. I knew how this would hurt her. It seemed that everything connected with my wedding was like a slap in the face to Mamá María.

"'*Muy bien*,' Mamá said bitterly. 'And your children will be American and can forget they have a grandmother living on this unfortunate island.' Though she had turned away from me, I could hear the pain in her voice.

"But still the wedding was beautiful. We had it at the church where the people sat according to their political affiliations, but when we got to the house where there was plenty of rum and food everybody forgot their differences for a little while. Mamá María was the perfect hostess. Two weeks later we were in New York where we were welcomed by Lorenzo Reyes. He was the son of one of Jorge's father's best friends in the army. The Reyes family had come to the United States early in the century to make cigars, then they branched out into other businesses. We were really lucky that your father got a job immediately."

"*Mas cafe, hija?*" My mother rose to pour herself another cup.

"No, thanks. Mami, you say you were lucky, but what about Papi's dream of owning a business of his own?"

My mother sighed. Mine is a moot question. We both know that my father did not make enough money to save for investments—not even for a house. My mother let me know that she had ended her story by taking our cups to the sink. The shadow of sadness had descended over her face again, but she was in control—I could tell by the way she had set her chin, the "iron jaw" I secretly called it. It meant that she had reached a final decision, taken a stand; whatever it was, for better or for worse, she would not budge.

"What a dream is for, *hija*, is to keep you going. That is the purpose of dreams for some people."

I started to leave the table since we had again reached that impasse where my language and hers do not meet. *My* dreams were going to come true. My dreams were plans, not some cloud-cuckooland fantasy. I was going to finish college. I planned on having a profession, not just a job. I would not settle like they did for the minimum of everything. I would leave her to her memories. I had books to read, work to do. But she stopped me with an open hand. Inside her palm was a chain with a medal I had seen around her neck all of my life. It is the Alta Gracia, Mother Mary as the Queen of Heaven, the one her mother gave her so many years ago in another world. She took my hand in hers and shut my fingers around the sharp medal of heavy gold in its chain. Tears began their way up to my eyes. For no reason at all, I recalled the young lovers dying in the cave. And I cried for them. Then I sat back down to let my mother put the gold chain around my neck. It would go with me into my own story.

Love and Vida

First Love

At fourteen and for a few years after, my concerns were focused mainly on the alarms going off in my body warning me of pain or pleasure ahead.

I fell in love, or my hormones awakened from their long slumber in my body, and suddenly the goal of my days was focused on one thing: to catch a glimpse of my secret love. And it had to remain secret, because I had, of course, in the great tradition of tragic romance, chosen to love a boy who was totally out of my reach. He was not Puerto Rican; he was Italian and rich. He was also an older man. He was a senior at the high school when I came in as a freshman. I first saw him in the hall, leaning casually on a wall that was the border line between girlside and boyside for under-classmen. He looked extraordinarily like a young Marlon Brando—down to the ironic little smile. The total of what I knew about the boy who starred in every one of my awkward fantasies was this: He was the nephew of the man who owned the supermarket on my block; he often had parties at his parents' beautiful home in the suburbs which I would hear about; this family had money (which came to our school in many ways)—and this last fact made my knees weak: He worked at the store near my apartment building on weekends and in the summer.

My mother could not understand why I became so eager to be the one sent out on her endless errands. I pounced on every opportunity from Friday to late

Saturday afternoon to go after eggs, cigarettes, milk (I tried to drink as much of it as possible, although I hated the stuff)—the staple items that she would order from the "American" store.

Week after week I wandered up and down the aisles, taking furtive glances at the stock room in the back, breathlessly hoping to see my prince. Not that I had a plan. I felt like a pilgrim waiting for a glimpse of Mecca. I did not expect him to notice me. It was sweet agony.

One day I did see him. Dressed in a white outfit like a surgeon; white pants and shirt, white cap, and (gross sight, but not to my love-glazed eyes) blood- smeared butcher's apron. He was helping to drag a side of beef into the freezer storage area of the store. I must have stood there like an idiot, because I remember that he did see me, he even spoke to me! I could have died. I think he said, "Excuse me," and smiled vaguely in my direction.

After that, I willed occasions to go to the supermarket. I watched my mother's pack of cigarettes empty ever so slowly. I wanted her to smoke them fast. I drank milk and forced it on my brother (although a second glass for him had to be bought with my share of Fig Newton cookies, which we both liked, but we were restricted to one row each). I gave my cookies up for love, and watched my mother smoke her L&Ms with so little enthusiasm that I thought (God, no!) that she might be cutting down on her smoking or maybe even giving up the habit. At this crucial time!

I thought I had kept my lonely romance a secret. Often I cried hot tears on my pillow for the things that kept us apart. In my mind there was no doubt that he would never notice me (and that is why I felt free to stare at him—I was invisible). He could not see me because I was a skinny Puerto Rican girl, a freshman who did not belong to any group he associated with.

At the end of the year I found out that I had not been invisible. I learned one little lesson about human nature—adulation leaves a scent, one that we are all equipped to recognize, and no matter how insignificant the source, we seek it.

Each June, the nuns at our school would always arrange for some cultural extravaganza. In my freshman year it was a Roman banquet. We had been studying Greek drama (as a prelude to church history—it was at a fast clip that we galloped through Sophocles and Euripides toward the early Christian martyrs), and our young, energetic Sister Agnes was in the mood for spectacle. She ordered the entire student body (a small group of under 300 students) to have our mothers make us togas out of sheets. She handed out a pattern on mimeo pages fresh out of the machine. I remember the intense smell of the alcohol on the sheets of paper, and how almost everyone in the auditorium brought theirs to their noses and inhaled deeply—mimeographed handouts were the school-day buzz that the new Xerox generation of kids is missing out on. Then, as the last couple of weeks of school dragged on, the city of Paterson becoming a concrete oven, and us wilting in our uncomfortable uniforms, we labored like frantic Roman slaves to build a splendid banquet hall in our small auditorium. Sister Agnes wanted a raised dais where the host and hostess would be regally enthroned.

She had already chosen our Senator and Lady from among our ranks. The Lady was to be a beautiful new student named Sophia, a recent Polish immigrant, whose English was still practically unintelligible, but whose features, classically perfect without a trace of makeup, enthralled us. Everyone talked about her gold hair cascading past her waist, and her voice which could carry a note right up to heaven in choir. The nuns wanted her for God. They kept saying that she had a vocation. We just looked at her in awe, and the boys seemed afraid of her. She just smiled and did as she was told. I don't know what she thought of it all. The main privilege of beauty is that others will do almost everything for you, including thinking.

Her partner was to be our best basketball player, a tall, red-haired senior whose family sent its many off-spring to our school. Together, Sophia and her senator looked like the best combination of immigrant genes our community could produce. It did not occur to me to ask then whether anything but their physical beauty qualified them for the starring roles in our production. I had the highest average in the church history class, but I was given the part of one of many "Roman citizens." I was to sit in front of the plastic fruit and recite a greeting in Latin along with the rest of the school when our hosts came into the hall and took their places on their throne.

On the night of our banquet, my father escorted me in my toga to the door of our school. I felt foolish in my awkwardly draped sheet (blouse and skirt required underneath). My mother had no great skill as a seamstress. The best she could do was hem a skirt or a pair of pants. That night I would have traded her for a peasant woman with a golden needle. I saw other Roman ladies emerging from their parents' cars looking authentic in sheets of material that folded over their bodies like the garments on a statue by Michelangelo. How did they do it? How was it that I always got it just slightly wrong? And worse, I believed that other people were just too polite to mention it. "The poor little Puerto Rican girl," I could hear them thinking. But in reality, I must have been my worst critic, self-conscious as I was.

Soon, we were all sitting at our circle of tables joined together around the dais. Sophia glittered like a golden statue. Her smile was beatific: a perfect, silent Roman lady. Her "senator" looked uncomfortable, glancing around at his buddies, perhaps waiting for the ridicule that he would surely get in the locker room later. The nuns in their black habits stood in the background watching us. What were they supposed to be, the Fates? Nubian slaves? The dancing girls did their modest little dance to tinny music from their finger cymbals, then the speeches were made. Then the grape vine "wine" was raised in a toast to the Roman Empire we all knew would fall within the week—before finals anyway.

All during the program I had been in a state of controlled hysteria. My secret love sat across the room from me looking supremely bored. I watched his every move, taking him in gluttonously. I relished the shadow of his eyelashes on his ruddy cheeks, his pouty lips smirking sarcastically at the ridiculous sight of our little play. Once he slumped down on his chair, and our sergeant-at-arms nun came over and tapped him sharply on his shoulder. He drew himself up slowly, with disdain. I loved his rebellious spirit. I believed myself still invisible to him in my "nothing" status as I looked upon my beloved. But towards the end of the evening, as we stood chanting our farewells in Latin, he looked straight across the room and into my eyes! How did I survive the killing power of those dark pupils? I trembled in a new way. I was not cold—I was burning! Yet I shook from the inside out, feeling light-headed, dizzy.

The room began to empty and I headed for the girls' lavatory. I wanted to relish the miracle in silence. I did not think for a minute that anything more would follow. I was satisfied with the enormous favor of a look from my beloved. I took my time, knowing that my father would be waiting outside for me, impatient, perhaps glowing in the dark in his phosphorescent white Navy uniform. The others would ride home. I would walk home with my father, both of us in costume. I wanted as few witnesses as possible. When I could no longer hear the crowds in the hallway, I emerged from the bathroom, still under the spell of those mesmerizing eyes.

The lights had been turned off in the hallway and all I could see was the lighted stairwell, at the bottom of which a nun would be stationed. My father would be waiting just outside. I nearly screamed when I felt someone grab me by the waist. But my mouth was quickly covered by someone else's mouth. I was being kissed. My first kiss and I could not even tell who it was. I pulled away to see that face not two inches away from mine. It was he. He smiled down at me. Did I have a silly expression on my face? My glasses felt crooked on my nose. I was unable to move or to speak. More gently, he lifted my chin and touched his lips to mine. This time I did not forget to enjoy it. Then, like the phantom lover that he was, he walked away into the darkened corridor and disappeared.

I don't know how long I stood there. My body was changing right there in the hallway of a Catholic school. My cells were tuning up like musicians in an orchestra, and my heart was a chorus. It was an opera I was composing, and I wanted to stand very still and just listen. But, of course, I heard my father's voice talking to the nun. I was in trouble if he had had to ask about me. I hurried down the stairs making up a story on the way about feeling sick. That would explain my flushed face and it would buy me a little privacy when I got home.

The next day Father announced at the breakfast table that he was leaving on a six-month tour of Europe with the Navy in a few weeks and, that at the end of the school year my mother, my brother, and I would be sent to Puerto Rico to stay for half a year at Mama's (my maternal grandmother's) house. I was devastated. This was the usual routine for us. We had always gone to Mama's to stay when Father was away for long periods. But this year it was different for me. I was in love, and . . . my heart knocked against my bony chest at this thought . . . he loved me too? I broke into sobs and left the table.

In the next week I discovered the inexorable truth about parents. They can actually carry on with their plans right through tears, threats, and the awful spectacle of a teenager's broken heart. My father left me to my mother, who impassively packed while I explained over and over that I was at a crucial time in my studies and that if I left my entire life would be ruined. All she would say is, "You are an intelligent girl, you'll catch up." Her head was filled with visions of *casa* and family reunions, long gossip sessions with her mama and sisters. What did she care that I was losing my one chance at true love?

In the meantime I tried desperately to see him. I thought he would look for me too. But the few times I saw him in the hallway, he was always rushing away. It would be long weeks of confusion and pain before I realized that the kiss was nothing but a little trophy for his ego. He had no interest in me other than as his adorer. He was flattered by my silent worship of him, and he had bestowed a kiss on me to please himself, and to fan the flames. I learned a lesson about the battle of the sexes then that I have never forgotten: The object is not always to win, but most times simply to keep your opponent (synonymous at times with "the loved one") guessing.

But this is too cynical a view to sustain in the face of that overwhelming rush of emotion that is first love. And in thinking back about my own experience with it, I can be objective only to the point where I recall how sweet the anguish was, how caught up in the moment I felt, and how every nerve in my body was involved in this salute to life.

Later, much later, after what seemed like an eternity of dragging the weight of unrequited love around with me, I learned to make myself visible and to relish the little battles required to win the greatest prize of all. And much later, I read and understood Albert Camus's statement about the subject that concerns both adolescent and philosopher alike: If love were easy, life would be too simple.

Vida

To a child, life is a play directed by parents, teachers, and other adults who are forever giving directions: "Say this," "Don't say that," "Stand here," "Walk this way," "Wear these clothes," and on and on and on. If we miss or ignore a cue, we are punished. And so we memorized the script of our lives as interpreted by our progenitors, and we learned not to extemporize too much: The world—our audience—likes the well-made play, with everyone in their places and not too many bursts of brilliance or surprises. But once in a while new characters walk onto the stage, and the writers have to scramble to fit them in, and for a while, life gets interesting.

Vida was a beautiful Chilean girl who simply appeared in the apartment upstairs with her refugee family one day and introduced herself into our daily drama.

She was tall, thin and graceful as a ballerina, with fair skin and short black hair. She looked like a gazelle as she bounded down the stairs from her apartment to ours the day she first came to our door to borrow something. Her accent charmed us. She said that she had just arrived from Chile with her sister, her sister's newborn baby girl, her sister's husband, and their grandmother. They were all living together in a one-bedroom apartment on the floor above us.

There must have been an interesting story of political exile there, but I was too young to care about that detail. I was immediately fascinated by the lovely Vida, who looked like one of the models in the fashion magazines that I, just turning twelve, had begun to be interested in. Vida came into my life during one of my father's long absences with the Navy, so that his constant vigilance was not a hindrance to my developing attachment to this vibrant human being. It was not a friendship—she was too much older than I and too self-involved to give me much in return for my devotion. It was more a Sancho Panza/Knight of La Mancha relationship, with me following her while she explored the power of her youth and beauty.

Vida wanted to be a movie star in Hollywood. That is why she had come to America, she said. I believed that she would be, although she spoke almost no English. That was my job, she said, to teach her to speak perfect English without an accent. She had finished secondary school in her country, and although she was only sixteen, she was not going to school in Paterson. She had other plans. She would get a job as soon as she had papers, save money, then she would leave for Hollywood as soon as possible. She asked me how far Hollywood was. I showed her the state of California in my geography book. She traced a line with her finger from New Jersey to the west coast and smiled. Nothing seemed impossible to Vida.

It was summer when I met Vida, and we spent our days in the small, fenced-in square lot behind our apartment building, avoiding going indoors as much as possible, since it was depressing to Vida to hear her family talking about the need to find jobs, to smell sour baby smells, or to be constantly lectured to by her obese grandmother, who sat like a great pile of laundry on a couch all day, watching shows on television which she did not understand. The brother-in-law frightened me a little with his intense eyes and his constant pacing. He spoke in whispers to his wife, Vida's sister, when I was around, as if he did not want me to overhear important matters, making me feel like an intruder. I didn't like to look at Vida's sister. She looked like a Vida who had been left out in the elements for too long: skin stuck to the bones. Vida did not like her family either. When I asked, she said that her mother was dead and that she did not want to speak of the past. Vida thought of only the future.

Once, when we were alone in her apartment, she asked me if I wanted to see her in a bathing suit. She went into the bathroom and emerged in a tight red one-piece suit. She reclined on the bed in a pose she had obviously seen in a magazine. "Do you think I am beautiful?" she asked me. I answered yes, suddenly overwhelmed by a feeling of hopelessness for my skinny body, bony arms and legs, flat chest. "Cadaverous," Vida had once whispered, smiling wickedly into my face after taking my head into her hands and feeling my skull so close to the surface. But right afterwards she had kissed my cheek, reassuring me that I would "flesh out" in a few years.

That summer my life shifted on its axis. Until Vida, my mother had been the magnetic force around which all my actions revolved. Since my father was away for long periods of time, my young mother and I had developed a strong symbiotic relationship, with me playing the part of interpreter and buffer to the world for her. I knew at an early age that I would be the one to face landlords, doctors, store clerks, and other "strangers" whose services we needed in my father's absence. English was my weapon and my power. As long as she lived in her fantasy that her exile from Puerto Rico was temporary and that she did not need to learn the language, keeping herself "pure" for her return to the island, then I was in control of our lives outside the realm of our little apartment in Paterson— that is, until Father came home from his Navy tours: Then the mantle of responsibility would fall on him. At times, I resented his homecomings, when I would suddenly be thrust back into the role of dependent which I had long ago outgrown—and not by choice.

But Vida changed me. I became secretive, and every outing from our apartment building—to get my mother a pack of L&Ms; to buy essentials at the drugstore or supermarket (which my mother liked to do on an as-needed basis); and, Vida's favorite, to buy Puerto Rican groceries at the bodega—became an adventure with Vida. She was getting restless living in such close quarters with her paranoid sister and brother-in-law. The baby's crying and the pervasive smells of dirty diapers drove her crazy, as did her fat grandmother's lethargy, which was disturbed only by the old woman's need to lecture Vida about her style of dress and her manners, which even my mother had started to comment on.

Vida was modeling herself on the go-go girls she loved to watch on dance shows on our television set. She would imitate their movements with me as her audience until we both fell on the sofa laughing. Her eye make-up (bought with my allowance) was dark and heavy, her lips were glossy with iridescent tan lipstick, and her skirts were riding higher and higher on her long legs. When we walked up the street on one of my errands, the men stared; the Puerto Rican men did more than that. More than once we were followed by men inspired to compose *piropos* for Vida—erotically charged words spoken behind us in stage whispers.

I was scared and excited by the trail of Vida's admirers. It was a dangerous game for both of us, but for me especially, since my father could come home unannounced at any time and catch me at it. I was the invisible partner in Vida's life; I was her little pocket mirror she could take out any time to confirm her beauty and her power. But I was too young to think in those terms; all I knew was the thrill of being in her company, being touched by her magical powers of transformation that could make a walk to the store a deliciously sinful escapade.

Then Vida fell in love. He was, in my jealous eyes, a Neanderthal, a big hairy man who drove a large black Oldsmobile recklessly around our block hour after hour just to catch a glimpse of Vida. He had promised to drive her to California, she confided to me. Then she started to use me as cover in order to meet him, asking me to take a walk with her, then leaving me to wait on a park bench or at the library for what seemed an eternity while she drove around with her muscle-bound lover. I became disenchanted with Vida, but remained loyal to her throughout the summer. Once in a while we still shared a good time. She loved to tell me in detail about her "romance." Apparently, she was not totally naive, and had managed to keep their passionate encounters within the limits of kissing and petting in the spacious backseat of the black Oldsmobile. But he was getting impatient, she told me, so she had decided to announce her engagement to her family soon. They would get married and go to California together. He would be her manager and protect her from the Hollywood "wolves."

By this time I was getting weary of Vida's illusions about Hollywood. I was glad when school started in the fall and I got into my starched blue jumper only to discover that it was too tight and too short for me. I had "developed" over the summer.

Life settled to our normal routine when we were in the States. This was: My brother and I went to Catholic school and did our lessons, our mother waited for our father to come home on leave from his Navy tours, and all of us waited to hear when we would be returning to Puerto Rico—which was usually every time Father went to Europe, every six months or so. Vida would sometimes come down to our apartment and complain bitterly about life with her family upstairs. They had absolutely refused to accept her fiancé. They were making plans to migrate elsewhere. She did not have work papers yet, but did not want to go with them. She would have to find a place to stay until she got married. She began courting my mother. I would come home to find them looking at bride magazines and laughing together. Vida hardly spoke to me at all.

Father came home in his winter blues and everything changed for us. I felt the almost physical release of the burden of responsibility for my family and allowed myself to spend more time doing what I liked to do best of all—read. It was a solitary life we led in Paterson, New Jersey, and both my brother and I became avid readers. My mother did too, although because she had little English, her fare was made up of Corín Tellado romances, which Schulze's drugstore carried, and the *Buenhogar* and *Vanidades* magazines that she received in the mail occasionally. But she read less and I more when Father came home. The ebb and flow of this routine was interrupted by Vida that year. With my mother's help she introduced herself into our family.

Father, normally a reticent man, suspicious of strangers by nature, and always vigilant about dangers to his children, also fell under Vida's spell. Amazingly, he agreed to let her come stay in our apartment until her wedding some months away. She moved into my room. She slept on what had been my little brother's twin bed until he got his own room, a place where I liked to keep my collection of dolls from around the world that my father had sent me. These had to be put in a box in the dark closet now.

Vida's perfume took over my room. As soon as I walked in, I smelled her. It got on my clothes. The nuns at my school commented on it since we were not allowed to use perfume or cosmetics. I tried to wash it off, but it was strong and pervasive. Vida tried to win me by taking me shopping. She was getting money from her boyfriend—for her trousseau—she said. She bought me a tight black skirt just like hers and a pair of shoes with heels. When she had me model it for my family, my father frowned and left the room silently. I was not allowed to keep these things. Since the man was never seen at our house, we did not know that Vida had broken the engagement and was seeing other men.

My mother started to complain about little things Vida did, or did not do. She did not help with housework, although she did contribute money. Where was she getting it? She did not bathe daily (a major infraction in my mother's eyes), but poured cologne over herself in quantities. She claimed to be at church too many times a week and came home smelling of alcohol, even though it was hard to tell because of the perfume. Mother was spreading her wings and getting ready to fight for exclusivity over her nest.

But, Father, surprising us all again, argued for fairness for the *señorita*. My mother made a funny "harrump" noise at that word, which in Spanish connotes virginity and purity. He said we had promised her asylum until she got settled and it was important that we send her out of our house in a respectable manner: married, if possible. He liked playing cards with her. She was cunning and smart, a worthy adversary.

Mother fumed. My brother and I spent a lot of time in the kitchen or living room, reading where the air was not saturated with "Evening in Paris."

Vida was changing. After a few months, she no longer spoke of Hollywood; she barely spoke to me at all. She got her papers and got a job in a factory sewing dungarees. Then, almost as suddenly as she had come into my life, she disappeared.

One afternoon I came home to find my mother mopping the floors strenuously with a pine cleaner, giving the apartment the kind of thorough scrubbing usually done as a family effort in the spring. When I went into my room, the dolls were back in their former place on the extra bed. No sign of Vida.

I don't remember discussing her parting much. Although my parents were fair, they did not always feel the need to explain or justify their decisions to us. I have always believed that my mother simply demanded her territory, fearing the growing threat of Vida's beauty and erotic slovenliness that was permeating her clean home. Or perhaps Vida found life with us as stifling as she had with her family. If I had been a little older, I would have learned more from Vida, but she came at a time when I needed security more than knowledge of human nature. She was a fascinating creature.

The last time I saw Vida's face it was on a poster. It announced her crowning as a beauty queen for a Catholic church in another parish. Beauty contests were held by churches as fundraisers at that time, as contradictory as that seems to me now: a church sponsoring a competition to choose the most physically attractive female in the congregation. I still feel that it was right to see Vida wearing the little tiara of fake diamonds in that photograph with the caption underneath: Vida wins!

About the Author

Judith Ortiz Cofer was born in Hormigueros, Puerto Rico. Her family moved to Paterson, New Jersey, soon thereafter, and she traveled back and forth between the island and New Jersey throughout her childhood. Her collection *An Island Like You: Stories from the Barrio* (Puffin) received the 1995 REFORMA/Pura Belpré Award for fiction and was named an ALA Best Book for Young Adults, a *School Library Journal* Best Book of the Year, and a *Horn Book* Fanfare title. Her other work includes the award-winning *Silent Dancing: A Partial Reminiscence of a Puerto Rican Childhood*, and the poetry collections *Terms of Survival* and *Reaching for the Mainland*.

Judith Ortiz Cofer is a professor of English and Creative Writing at the University of Georgia in Athens. She and her husband have one daughter.

Visit her Web site at **parallel.park.uga.edu/~jcofer.**

Acknowledgments

Several pieces in this volume first appeared in book form in the author's *Terms of Survival* (Arte Público Press, 1987) and *Silent Dancing: A Partial Remembrance of a Puerto Rican Childhood* (Arte Público Press, 1990); "Kennedy in the Barrio" was first published in *Microfiction: An Anthology of Really Short Stories,* edited by Jerome Stern (Norton, 1996). "Volar" was first published in *In Short: A Collection of Brief Creative Nonfiction,* Judith Kitchen and Mary Paumier Jones, editors (Norton, 1996).